THE Fall

(Book Three)

Thou Shall Not Fear

By

Sabrina B. Scales

Dedication

This and every story I release this year is dedicated to my fourth decade on earth. I have been blessed beyond measure. I am grateful for all of you. I am living my wildest dreams and the best is yet to come!

Description

Even the saved struggle when navigating their way through love. This much could definitely be said for the Fold Family's oldest child, Angela.

Perfection was the main objective when it came to Angela. She was stubborn, strong-willed, and completely incapable of relinquishing control, at times risking her own happiness to preserve the image of what others thought she should be.

But just like glass, perfect images crack. And what's left can either be cleaned up or left for somebody to step in. Angela must take it upon herself to figure out which way to go after leaving a toxic marriage. And she may or may not find refuge in an equally stubborn alpha-male by the name of Damien Christopher Briscoe.

Take this journey of acceptance, sacrifice, and necessary surrender in this story of love unearthed in the final installment of The Fold!

One

He came to me at a time in my life when everything seemed so urgent. Nearing thirty with no husband and no kids, not even a plant in my window to prove that I could sustain a life outside of my own, I could literally hear the clock ticking and I obsessed over it every day. It seems so crazy now, thinking back on the lengths I'd gone through to create something perfect that was everything but. And sadly, I'd probably do it all again, because that's how obsession works.

Perfection.

It's the thing I'm obsessed with. A lifelong attempt to follow in the footsteps of the most amazing man God ever created. Never wanting to let him down. Never wanting him to feel like he'd dropped the ball while raising me. Never, ever going to bed at night without dropping to my knees to pray that the Lord understood how grateful I was that he'd chosen me to be the eldest daughter of Pastor Chadwick Fold Sr.

While most little girls aspired to be just like their mothers, my sole purpose in life was to move people the way that my father did. I didn't necessarily want to become a minister, but the feeling he delivered. The undeniable shift in the atmosphere when he entered a room, I wanted that. Might even say I needed it. And it was my assumption that the only way to attain it was to be as close to perfect as humanly possible. To fall in love, be fruitful and multiply. All the traditional things that other Christian women did. It's amazing how focused one can become on a thing, ignoring all of the signs screaming for us to stop and pay attention. I was willing to risk it all and did in so many ways because the suffering didn't matter if, in the end, I got to be more like him.

The Legacy of *The Fold* meant more to me than almost anything. Folks looked up to my father because he was a good man. A man who chose the path of righteousness when alternative paths would've been much easier to follow. There was a calling on his life, one that he told me couldn't be ignored. I admired his obedience, his sureness, and his strength. But above all, I admired the simplicity with which he delivered the word, setting souls free one Sunday at a time, providing hope where all was lost.

Once, when I was little, I called him a magician after watching him invoke the Holy Spirit during a revival on the lawn in an apartment complex. There was an elderly lady there who'd been stricken with cancer and screamed about how God had turned his back on her by not providing her with a cure. I'll never forget my father's words as he left the makeshift podium that he'd built in his father's shed when he was thirteen years old. He walked right up to that woman and went down on his knees wearing a pair of dark denim Levi's and a crisp dress shirt. He grabbed her by her wrinkled hands then looked into her sunken eyes, tapping into the very vein of God's own heart and said, *"God will never leave you, nor will he forsake you. His power is abundant, merciful and sure. Though our days be numbered, they are his by default. Be ye thankful for the days. Be ye blessed, no matter how few."*

Seemingly simple words sent the woman bursting into tears. Her hands trembled in my father's grasp and every eye on the lawn was on them. She did not stand. She did not shout. And her gray skin did not gain pigment. But the Holy Spirit was present in the tears falling from her eyes. There was a shift in her that may very well have replaced sorrow with joy in her final days.

The very next week, that woman passed away, and my father eulogized her at the request of one of her neighbors. She said that she'd seen a change in the woman, Ms. Bobbi, toward the end of her illness, that didn't seem normal since she'd had such strong faith. She said she was happy that my father came to their complex on that day. Sometimes we need to be reminded of God's grace in the midst of our storms. Praying for miracles and more days isn't always the solution. Death is only the foreseeable ending to our physical stage in life.

That happened years ago and many times after. So often that it seemed like second nature to my father but was always magical to me. As I got older, I wanted so badly to ask him if he could sprinkle that magic on me. But I was scared that his revelation might be that I'd grow old in a house full of cats.

Fear of cats.

That's what led me to the arms of a man who rejected monogamy. He gave me all the signs I needed, and I convinced myself that I could fix him. Because that's what you do when you're desperate. Those are the depths that my heart was willing to travel in search of perfection that never really existed.

"You can't keep doing this, Penny." My baby brother sat next to me at the head of my bed, holding and feeding a child that I couldn't even look at because I hated her father more than a saved woman should, even after I'd prayed about it.

Chad was the only one who knew about my husband's transgressions and promised not to tell a soul because he knew how important the perfect picture was to me.

"I don't have a choice." I flipped my legs off the side of the bed and footed into the bathroom to empty my bladder. I'd been living off of chicken broth and fruit juices for the past eight weeks since giving birth to Patience, fasting and praying in hopes that it would change the way I felt.

"Your choice is right here." He said, taking the bottle out of my baby's mouth and sitting it on the nightstand. "I don't mind being here because I love you and I love Boogie. But this ain't healthy."

"I'm trying, Chad." I rejoined them on the bed, sitting in awe of how seamlessly he propped her little body up against his shoulder and patted her back until she burped when I could barely bring myself to do it.

"You're fasting and praying." He cut his eyes at me. "And that'd be fine if you were prepping for a job interview. But this is your baby, not some new gig."

"You don't think I know that? I know that!" I was almost in tears because we'd had this conversation so many times in the past few weeks it felt redundant. "And I feel like shit for not being able to look at her and feel all warm and fuzzy like I thought I would. Like the mamas on the pamphlets at the doctor's office."

"Maybe you were looking at the wrong pamphlets." Chad sighed, craning his neck to look down at his niece who had already fallen asleep against his chest. "I'm sure they have help for this. You just need to find it."

"And what am I supposed to say to this help? *That I love my baby but can't stand to look at her because she has her father's eyes? That I'm not even sure I wanna be her mother?*"

"Yeah. All of that." His eyes widened as he cradled Patience's head in the palm of his hand and brought her down from his shoulder with a gentleness I'd never seen before. "And then they'll tell you that it's perfectly normal. That you're not the only one and that they can help you."

"Chad," I called him by his nickname instead of calling him Chadwick like I usually did because he'd been the only one I allowed to be there during what had to be the most trying time in my life.

"Yeah?" He looked back at me after leaving the bed to lay Patience in her bassinet.

With emotions curling in my throat and a heaviness weighing deep down in my chest, I whimpered words that I never thought I'd say. But they were the only ones true enough to encompass what I was feeling.

"I'm scared." I sat straight up catching his eyes halfway across my bedroom.

Then I broke down. For the first time since leaving the hospital with my baby girl without her father by my side to offer the support I needed, I came undone and my baby brother was there to catch me without judgment and without hesitance.

"I know." He said, hurrying over and sitting on the side of the bed, roping his arm around my shoulder and pulling me in against the side of him. "And I'll be here until you're not." He planted a kiss on my forehead, forever changing the way I saw him. Forever confirming the presence of God *in* him.

"Hand me my grandbaby!" Mama was over the moon excited to see Patience on Sunday mornings, clothed in ruffles from head to toe thanks to Chad coming over early to help me get her dressed.

Nobody really noticed my husband's absence, or at least they didn't mention it. And if they did, I'd simply put them off with an excuse about him working long hours.

"She's getting so chubby, Penny." Mama took Patience from Chad and cradled her in the bend of her arm as we gathered in front of Daddy's study before sunrise service began.

"That's 'cause she's always eating." Chad chimed in like he always did, covering for the less than enthusiastic response that I didn't have the energy to fake.

"I see." Mama smiled down at Patience. "You know, I didn't expect you to take this uncle business so seriously. You seem to know more about your niece than her own mama." Her eyes swept between me and Chad before returning to Patience.

"It's a tough job but somebody's gotta do it." Chad joked, trying his best to lighten the mood because it was rarely ever light between me and my mother.

"I know things about her," I said defensively. "Chad's been a big help but he's not her father."

"I didn't say he was." Mama returned. "And speaking of which, where is Paul? We haven't seen him here in a month of Sundays."

"He's working." I quickly replied.

"Well, there are only so many hours in a day. When's he gonna find time to fellowship with his family?" Mama asked a logical question, but all I heard was judgment.

"We have bills, Mama. Sometimes sacrifices have to be made."

"Well, forgive me if I'm wrong, but I don't think the Lord should be sacrificial." She widened her eyes at me, and I knew that she was right. I'd said the exact same words to myself in the mirror when I stepped out of the shower that morning.

But, "The Lord is not being sacrificed. That's why I'm here with our daughter." Was what I said instead, defending a man who was no closer to being at work than the sun was to setting on our front porch. There's no telling where he was. I hadn't heard from him in two days and probably wouldn't hear from him for two more.

"Well, Amen to that." She digressed, propping Patience up on her shoulder as my father stepped out of the study wearing a royal blue robe that had always been considered a mystical garment to me.

"Everything alright out here? Looks like I walked into something?" Daddy's eyes slid between me and my mother before landing on Chad where he'd typically get his answer.

"Everything's fine, Pops." Chad clapped Daddy on the shoulder. "We just need the word, that's all."

"Well, I can help you with that." Pops grinned, planting a kiss on Mama's cheek, Patience's cheek then mine before we followed him into the sanctuary and prepared to receive the word.

I managed to make it through my younger sister, Jada and The Tabernacle Choir singing *"Total Praise"* without breaking down which seldom happened because that song carried so much with it. My soul was aching with all that I'd been carrying. And it felt like any minute, I'd be losing what was left of my mind. I looked to the left at my brother rocking my baby and a lump formed in my throat that I quickly swallowed down.

"Good morning Tabernacle." Daddy's voice swept away all the worries crowding my mind.

"Good morning." The church returned in unison, smiling, nodding and getting situated in their seats.

"It is a good day to be in the House of the Lord. Amen?" He went on, receiving and accepting almost enough Amens in return.

"Aww, we can do better than that, Tabernacle." My father wasn't pleased until the banners flanking the choir stand were waving from the vibrations of unified responses. "If the Lord woke you up and set you on your way this morning, you oughta be glad to shout Amen for all that He has done!"

"Amen!" We all shouted ten times louder bringing a smile to his handsome face and a bigger one to mine.

Patience wiggled in Chad's arms in response to the shouting. But she didn't cry one bit. Never did while we were at church.

"Amen." My father said, pleased with the congregation's response. "Now that we're all awake." He joked, sending scattered laughter from the front pew to the back. "The Lord sat a word in my spirit this morning. And I'll admit, I didn't quite understand where he was taking me with it. You see things can get a little cryptic when you're leaning to your own understanding, Church. So, I had to... I had to come up out of myself, Amen? Had to push back from my desk and ask the Lord to just...to just sit inside me. I don't always have the right words. I don't always know what to do. But God does."

Heads nodded, voices uttered agreement, and a few of the pews creaked as folks settled into the spirit.

"Many of you are aware that the Lord blessed me and my wife with three beautiful children." Daddy's eyes scanned from the choir stand where Jada was sitting, down to the front pew at me and Chad. "Even saw fit to give me a grandbaby that sits right through Sunday service without making a sound. Amen." He smiled as every eye in the church tried to find Patience who was already fast asleep in her uncle's arms.

"I'm grateful for my children." Daddy nodded, smile fading into something more serious. Sentimental even. "They're not perfect. They haven't always made the best decisions. And I won't call names, but one of 'em owes me twenty dollars for a lunch he invited me to then conveniently forgot his wallet at home." He cut his eyes at Chad and everybody started laughing.

"That's alright, son." He chuckled. "We're having Outback on you this evening, Amen?" Chad shook his head and grinned as an entire row of young ladies' eyes stuck to him like glue, as usual.

"Amen, just like our children." Daddy continued as the congregation calmed down. "We, God's children, we let our Father down sometimes." He planted his hands on either side of the podium and straightened his back.

"And I'm not just talking about coming up short on lunch money. I'm talking about breaking promises, Tabernacle. Finding ourselves in binds so tight that only the love of God can bring us out. And we promise him things. We, we, we get so bound up in desperation that we swear to God that if he pulls us out of this mess, we won't do it again. Somebody get where I'm goin' out there?"

"Yes!" Sister Grace, a well-known alcoholic who had lost and found the Lord at least twelve times in the past year, shouted all by herself.

"Amen. We take advantage of God's forgiveness because he is our Father." Daddy went on. "It's easy to make a promise when you're sitting in ICU with tubes running here and there because you just couldn't pass on one more slice of white cake with buttercream icing and your sugar shot through the roof. I'm talking to somebody this morning!" He looked out into the crowd for a witness and got a dozen shouts of encouragement.

"It ain't much of a challenge to tell God that you won't touch another drop of Hennessey when you need him to come bail you outta jail for that third DUI. Have I gone too far, church?" Daddy straightened his back, cutting his eyes at everybody and nobody in particular.

"Oh, Tabernacle we get too comfortable." His voice softened but his delivery did not. "And the good thing about God is that even though he knows our hearts. Even though he knows the likelihood of us falling right back into sin, He forgives us still. You know why?" He planted his hands on either side of his Bible and said. "Because somebody already paid the price."

With a deep breath that caused his chest to rise and fall, he flipped open his Bible, bringing those familiar with his routine to their feet. Patience was still sound asleep in Chad's arms, seemingly lulled by the sound of her grandfather's booming baritone delivering the word of God. He had arrived at the fruit, and it was finally time to be fed.

"If the Lord has blessed you with legs to stand, won't you come and go with me to the book of James, first chapter verses two through four and twelve."

My father only used the Bible as a point of reference, and once he saw the first word, he didn't even need to look down at it. I'd watched him study the words he'd be speaking to the congregation so thoroughly that at times, he said it was difficult to see the line between God's words and his own. He said that was the testament of a true man of faith. Being so completely drenched in the word that it became a part of you.

He read, *""My brethren, count it all joy when ye fall into divers temptation: 3 Knowing this, that the trying of your faith worketh patience 4 But let patience have her perfect work, that ye may be perfect and entire, wanting nothing 12 Blessed is the man that endureth temptation: for when he is tried, he shall receive the crown of life, which the Lord hath promised to them that love him."*

"Tabernacle, I want you to look at your neighbor, and say, neighbor,"

"Neighbor," The entire congregation followed his lead.

"In order to pick something up," He said, straightening his glasses as the congregation repeated,

"You gotta put something down." His shoulders relaxed as they shouted the last string of words then settled into their seats.

"God is a forgiving God. We know this." He said. "Many of us wouldn't be sitting here today if he wasn't, and Pastor Fold is not exempt from that truth. Amen?"

"Amen." We all nodded.

"But you see, His forgiveness is not the issue." He continued. "Amen. The issue is what we do with it. How we act in God's face after he's freed us from whatever was binding us. See many of us don't know what to do with forgiveness. We think being washed clean means that it's okay to go get dirty again 'cause God'll clean us right back up like he always does if we acknowledge his presence and repent. But don't you know, Tabernacle, that there is always a purpose in being washed clean? That there is a blessing on the other side of deliverance that you might never see because you're rushing back to the one thing that blocked your path?"

He gave us a moment to reflect on those words. To digest them and apply our own issues to the scenario. And when the moment was right, when eyes started to raise from focusing on their laps and pens were done jotting down his exact words to be read over and over again, he continued on.

"God is not man that he would lie, Tabernacle. Even though we lie to him each and every day, he is still there waiting to make good on his promises. But he can't give us the desires of our hearts if we refuse to do the work. If we refuse to break free from the bondage of sin and step into what we rightfully deserve. My God!"

Daddy stepped from behind the podium because that's what he did when the spirit swelled up in him so big that he literally needed more space.

"Keeping our promises to God isn't always easy. I know." He said, holding a Bible in one hand and a cloth in the other. "The flesh is weak. Always has been and always will be." A few folks shouted Amen loud enough to validate that the words were meant just for them.

"But we are more than flesh." Daddy panned the congregation, careful not to miss the crown of a single head. "Just as sure as the skin covering your bones, there's room inside of every one of us for the Holy Spirit to reside if you'd just let Him in. Let him pour into you when you're weak. Let him pour into you when you're sick. Let him pour into you when that buttermilk biscuit is calling your name and your glucose levels are already too high. Show some restraint, Tabernacle. You're more than a puppet for the Devil to pull in all these directions that contradict the calling God has on your life. Stand firm in your faith and do for God what you said you would do!" He shouted and I leaped up from my seat, tears trickled down my face and I could feel all that had been holding onto me being ripped away like cheap fabric.

My arms flew into the air, held in place by the Spirit and the Spirit alone. My back bowed and unfamiliar syllables took over my mouth, flowing from me like lyrics to a song that I'd never sang and likely wouldn't remember the words to. In my peripheral, I could see my mother hovering over me with a fan and Chad had slid out of the way still holding Patience in his arms. It could have been minutes, hours or days before the warmth that covered me pulled away and left be bare. But however long the feeling lasted, I was better having stood in it.

The rest of the service took place in my absence as the ushers escorted me to the sitting area at the back of the church to gather myself and have some water. I couldn't remember ever being so taken over. It's like one minute I was perfectly fine, happily celebrating the only thing that seemed to bring me joy. And before I knew it, I was engulfed in what can only be described as an out of body experience. My movements were not my own. The voice in my head was not my own. The climate around me had changed and there was no one else in the entire congregation. Just me, my feelings, and God.

Mama, Daddy, Chad, and Jada came back to check on me after the services were over and I could hardly find the words to let them know what I'd just experienced. But it was in that moment that my eyes connected with the little girl I'd shared my body with for forty whole weeks and I finally saw her as more than an object to be fed, clothed and attended to.

I saw love.

I saw my *daughter.*

I saw the truth in my situation and realized that if the dynamic of my family was ever going to get better, I needed to see it for what it was, take it to God, wait for him to tell me what to do and then do it.

Two

Two years later…

"I want a divorce."

God had told me two years prior, right there on that pew, that this was what I needed to do but all I could see was how imperfect it would look for me to dissolve a marriage in such a short amount of time. I never questioned the Lord's voice as much as I had in those twenty-four months. But the more I prayed, the clearer it became that changing this man was never an option.

"What brought you to this?" Paul, the man I'd been fool enough to marry after purposely getting pregnant to trap him and hopefully transform him into the man I so desired asked. "I mean aside from the fact that this was a stupid idea in the first place." He was always so casual about the situation. Didn't give a damn and made it a point to let me know every chance he got.

"I'm tired." I continued stuffing things in Patience's backpack. I'd gone from not knowing how to love my baby at two months old to not being able to imagine my life without the two-year-old cutie that was always attached to my hip.

"And I'm sure you are too." I continued, looking up at the man who'd been a decent father to our daughter and absolutely nothing to me.

"Yeah, I am." He nodded his head, big ass nose upsetting me because he was still able to breathe through it. "So, when do we get started?"

"Soon," I replied. "I just need to set some things straight first."

"What, you scared to tell your family?"

"God, here we go with this." I blew out a breath, sliding the baby's bag up on my shoulder and preparing to wake her from her nap so we could go and have lunch with Jada.

"What? It's the only thing that ever holds you back." He shrugged his bony shoulders, leaning on the kitchen island and biting into a green apple.

"You don't understand."

"Yeah, I do. I understand that I've been held hostage for two years because you're scared to tell your folks you're in a loveless marriage." He chewed those words down with his apple and what's sadder than what he said was the fact that it was true.

And of course, I didn't respond because the truth hurt. It always did, coming from Paul. He'd stayed the course and agreed to live under the same roof although our marriage was over before it even started. But he never passed on the opportunity to throw it in my face that I was wasting all my good years on a lie and dragging him and the baby along with me.

"Anyway, I'll probably be gone when y'all get back." He stood straight and dropped the core of the apple in the trash can.

"Good." I nodded, passing him and heading down the hallway to our daughter's room. "You should probably start looking for permanent residence. Maybe *Nedra* can help you find something." I shouted down the hall.

I could hear his feet hurrying behind me. It was always the same scene. Some chick sends a text looking for *"Darrell"* and I reply telling her she got the wrong number knowing full-well she hadn't because *Darrell* was his alias. The first time it happened it was some chick named Nedra and there'd been a dozen since then before and after we took our vows but for some reason, her name was etched in my memory. They say the first one always is.

"Don't worry, I haven't been going through your phone." I took a deep breath, turning to face him as I stood in front of Patience's door. "I don't wanna hold you hostage anymore, Paul. It's your life. I just... I was...crazy to think that I could change you. Or that I could change anybody for that matter. You're not a robot, you're a whore. And you have the right to be that."

"Wait, what?" He squinted. It was true, but I don't think he was prepared to hear it from my lips.

"I'm not judging you." I leaned against the door. "I don't even hate you."

"And you shouldn't. This shit is your fault."

"Paul, you're a grown-ass man. And I know I can be demanding, but if you didn't wanna be here you could've left a long time ago. But you didn't. And you know why you didn't? Because you benefitted from this arrangement just as much as I did."

"How so?" He had the nerve to ask, standing before me with his arms folded across his chest, wide ass nostrils flaring open enough to march an elephant up each hole.

"*How so?* Are you serious right now?" I smirked. "Do you honestly believe that you would've gotten hired on with the largest engineering firm in Houston had my father not put in a word for you? You can't be that delusional."

"All your pops did was drop my name. I kept the job by knowing what the fuck I'm doing so you can save that."

"You know what else I can save? My *breath*." I wrapped my hand around the doorknob to our baby's door. "Please don't be here when we get home tonight. The sooner you get out of here the better."

"I couldn't agree more." He sucked his teeth, backing away and heading off down the hallway before I pushed the door open and got Patience together.

"Penny?"

"Huh?"

"Are you deaf? Boogie's been yelling for you to look at that bird for two minutes."

"No, I'm...I'm sorry, baby." I followed my baby's finger to a red bird that had landed on the fence across from the picnic table that me, her, and Jada were sitting at. "What color is that bird, Boogie?" I asked, not at all surprised when she shouted *"Red!"* and started clapping. She was as smart as a whip and would be enrolled in pre-k had it not been for the stupid age policy.

"Are you okay?" Jada asked after sucking down a few ounces of green tea.

"What? Yeah. Why wouldn't I be?" I smirked, pulling a wet wipe from Penny's backpack and cleaning the organic pistachio ice cream that Jada'd insisted she have a scoop of from her chin.

"I don't know. That's why I'm asking." Jada darted her eyes at me, long chocolate ponytail blowing in the breeze.

"I'm fine, *rejected detective.* I'm just tired. Can I be tired?" I bucked my eyes.

"You can *be* whatever you want. Especially honest when your sister's asking you a question that she already knows the answer to."

"Jada, I don't—"

"Where is he?" She cut me off, handing Patience the bright green spoon she'd been reaching for to dig back into the ice cream she'd abandoned to bird-watch.

"Where is who?" I rolled my eyes, tossing the soiled wet wipe into the trash can beside our table.

"Don't play with me. You know damn well who."

"He's working. And why are you always asking me about him? You wanna take him off my hands or something?"

Of all my family members, Jada'd been pressing me the most about Paul's constant absence. I was able to keep the others at bay for the most part but this one. This one was nosey.

"I wouldn't take Paul if he came with an eight-inch dick and a private island." She quickly replied. "I just wanna know why you keep acting like everything is cool when your mood says otherwise. I haven't laid eyes on the dude in months. Did you kill him? Is he buried in the back yard? Is that why you're all shifty and shit?"

"First of all, watch your mouth." I raised a finger. "Your niece is a sponge. She told Miss Ling at daycare that she needed a drink because her nerves were bad yesterday. Any idea where she got that from?"

"Umm..."

"Exactly." I snapped.

"Whatever. You still didn't answer my question." She popped a piece of waffle cone in her mouth and crunched with her mouth wide open, knowing how much it annoyed me.

"I didn't kill anybody, crazy," I answered. "He's just working a lot. I don't know why that's so hard to believe."

I also didn't know why it was so hard to just tell the truth. That my marriage was a failure and I wasn't as perfect as everybody thought I was. If anybody'd be understanding it would be my own sister. She hadn't had the best track record with relationships herself. And forgiveness was kind of her thing. She'd been the only one of us to forgive our mother for ending a thirty-one-year marriage with our father to run off into the sunset with a woman who looked like a Manny Fresh.

So confusing.

"It's not." She dabbed the corners of her mouth with a napkin. "Or at least it wouldn't be if we were talking about a few days or even a few weeks. But *months*, Penny? He hasn't been to church with you and Boogie for months. Look, if there's something going on, something you need to vent about, just tell me. You don't have to go through this alone. Is he hitting you? Is he hitting Boogie? Penny, please tell me that big-nosed mother fu—"

"Jadalynn, stop!" I almost yelled, drawing attention from a couple passing by walking their dog. "Nobody is hitting anybody, okay? Me and Boogie are fine. Me and *Paul* are fine. And I'd appreciate it if you'd drop this investigation. It's getting annoying."

"I'm sorry. I'm just—"

"Concerned. I know. And while I appreciate your concern, it's not necessary. Seriously."

I flipped my legs over the side of the bench and stood up to dust peanuts and other fixings from my fudge sundae off my lap.

"Would you stop looking at me like that?" I darted my eyes to my sister who looked like she didn't believe a word I'd said.

"Yeah. As soon as you start telling me the truth." She stood up and dusted herself off. "Where did we go wrong? You used to tell me everything."

"We haven't gone wrong." I tried my best to assure her. "I swear." I looked straight into her eyes, gripping her hand when she rounded the table to collect our trash and drop it in the trash can.

"Okay." She shrugged. "Whatever you say."

I knew that didn't mean she'd accepted what I said. It actually meant the exact opposite. But I couldn't tell her the truth. Not yet. Because she wasn't ready for it and neither was I.

Three

It was over.

All disputes had been resolved and after two years and six months, my fragile marriage was over. I didn't leave the house for anything that didn't involve work, Boogie or church, and it was all I could do not to break down in front of people who had no idea the turmoil I was going through. Paul and I had agreed on joint-custody which meant that he'd have Boogie every other weekend leaving me two days alone to sulk. I wouldn't say that I missed him because there wasn't much to miss, but there was a void that he'd been able to fill less than a fourth of when he was around and now, even that was empty.

Breaking the news to my family would've been at the top of my list had it not been for the recent divorce of my parents and the fact that I was still waving a flag of perfection. I couldn't let it go; had lost sleep imagining what life would be like if people saw me as a failure. So, I kept it tucked close to my chest until it became so heavy that I had to let it go.

One night after Paul had come by to drop Patience off after picking her up from daycare, I convinced him to come over to my father's for dinner since they hadn't seen him in a while. We went back and forth before he finally gave in, making me promise to just tell them already because he was tired of playing games. I agreed to the deal, giving no specifics on the date, and we walked into Pastor Fold's abode as a three-part unit with Patience smiling like it was Christmas morning making me feel extremely guilty for getting her hopes up about me and her daddy.

"Well, would you look what the cat dragged in!" Daddy answered the door wearing a smoke-gray sweater, slacks and a smile as wide as the front of his truck.

"Hey, Paw Paw!" Patience released mine and Paul's hands to rush over and embrace her grandfather.

"Hey, Boogie Bear!" He leaned over and swooped her up into his arms. "Did the tooth fairy come by and pay for this tooth yet?" He asked, directing his attention to the open space at the front of her mouth.

"No, sir." She replied, smiling wide. "I left it at Daddy's house. She might not have his address. Daddy, did you give the tooth fairy your address?" Patience squealed and I almost melted into the damn floor.

"I… umm…"

"She just lost it last night." I cut in to save Paul from stuttering himself deeper into questioning. "At Granny Martha's. She must be confused."

"I'm not confused, Mommy. I was at Daddy's house. You're gonna confuse the tooth fairy."

I was so damned nervous I started itching under my arms. I never thought I'd be ratted out by my three-year-old daughter.

"You know what," Daddy swooped in, no doubt noticing the sweat beading on my forehead. "I think the old tooth fairy that used to collect mommy, Jada, and Uncle Chad's teeth might still stop by here from time to time. Why don't you give him a call?"

Daddy's eyes slid from Patience to me. And I was stuck in place. Was he aiding and abetting?

"I… Ummm…"

"I just shot him a text." Chad popped up behind Daddy, having walked in on the conversation.

"Uncie Chad!" Patience screamed. She would abandon anybody to go to her uncle Chad.

"Thank you." I mouthed to my baby brother who was always saving me from the messes I found myself in.

He nodded and rubbed his thumbs and fingers together, signaling that he expected to be financially compensated for this elaborate tooth fairy scheme.

"You should just tell 'em." Paul and I sat side by side on the sofa in the living room. My eyes traveled from Patience on the floor drawing on her tablet with Chad, to Jada on the phone probably shooting risky text messages to her newly rekindled lover, Andrew.

"Tell us what?" I assumed my sister couldn't hear Paul since she seemed so focused on her cell. But I was wrong. Jada's level of nosey-ness knew no boundaries.

"Nothing," I replied before Paul got a chance to.

"It didn't sound like *nothing*," Jada smirked, glancing up from her phone. "Paul, what y'all hiding? You got my sister pregnant again?"

"Jada!" I shrieked.

"What? Boogie needs a sibling." She shrugged. "Look at who she's playing with. You think that's healthy?"

"Excuse me?" Chad looked up at Jada, flicking a piece of Chex mix, hitting her on the forehead.

"I'm just sayin'." Jada picked the piece of pretzel off her shirt and popped it in her mouth. "There were three of us and you see how well we turned out."

"That's a terrible example." I rolled my eyes on a sigh. "And I'm not pregnant. Not even close."

I was so frustrated with the whole thing. Especially now that I'd dragged the baby into the lie. I was this close to just blurting it out. Consequences be damned.

"We're divorced." Paul must've been reading my mind for the first time ever in our damn relationship. I considered putting up a fight but decided it wasn't worth it. They'd find out eventually anyway so why not just rip off the band-aide.

"It's about time." Jada didn't bite her tongue.

"What? Damn." Chad looked back.

"Language." I scorned knowing Patience's ears were always seeking new words to embarrass me with.

"What's *duh-borced*, Daddy?" Patience asked without looking up from the butterfly she was sketching. And all I could do was cover my face with my hand.

"It's nothin', baby." He replied, shoving his hands in his pockets. "Grown-up stuff." God, I prayed she accepted that because I was nowhere near ready to explain why Daddy hadn't been sleeping under the same roof. I hoped she'd just get used to it and grow into our new normal.

Luckily, God was listening that night. Patience dropped the subject and Daddy didn't damn me to hell when I went into his office to break the news. One chain had been broken. A heavy one that was breaking me down day by day. I was free to live in a new truth that was imperfect but mine and that was surprisingly more relieving than I'd expected.

<h1 style="text-align:center">Four</h1>

"Say, if you don't wanna end up back where you came from, you're gonna have to get a better watch."

"I use my phone."

"Do I look like I'm in the mood for *Amateur Night*, bro? Like is that why you think I've been sitting at this desk for the past twenty minutes waiting for your irresponsible ass to show up?"

I'd had my share of hopeless clients at this desk. But Dupre wasn't one of them.

Which was why it pissed me off when he showed up to his weekly visits late.

"My bad, Mr. Briscoe." He apologized once he realized I wasn't in the mood for joking. At twenty-two years old, he'd landed himself in a position where bullshitting wasn't something he could do often, or at all as far as I was concerned.

"Yeah, *your bad*." I slid my eyes from him to the deep drawer under my desk where I retrieved a thick, plastic specimen cup. "You know what to do. Clyde's waiting for you."

"Bro, does he really have to be in there?" Dupre smacked his lips, snatching the cup from my desk and standing from his seat. "I think that nigga gay."

"Clyde's sexual preference ain't got shit to do with you pissing in that cup. And if you hadn't come in here last week pregnant with puppies, he wouldn't have to go in there with you in the first place."

"Man, I hit *one* joint." He rolled his eyes up to the side.

"Yeah. One joint that had you collecting piss from a pit bull and could've cost you your freedom, *again*." I hiked a brow. "Go piss so I can wrap up this paperwork and get the hell outta here."

"Why, you got somewhere to be?" He smirked. My life was mostly bland when I wasn't working for others.

"Once again you're worried about shit that has nothing to do with you leaving human piss in that cup. Go." I pointed toward the door. Dupre grinned and took off with Clyde waiting there to escort him while I crossed my fingers that this cat didn't come in with fake or dirty piss because the last place he needed to be was back behind bars.

"So, he was clean? He said he was clean. But you know how Dupre lies. I used to be able to tell by looking at him but now that he's a hardened criminal and shit, I think he perfected the art of lying straight to my face."

Dupre's older sister, Nelly, had been his legal guardian since their mother was thrown in prison for a third strike drug charge when Nelly was eighteen and Dupree was thirteen. She'd done the best she could under the circumstances. Even pushed him to finish high school. But as is likely the case where we're from, the streets got ahold of Dupre and landed him in the wrong place at the wrong time.

"He was clean," I assured her over the phone, hurrying to my car to get to my next gig.

"Are you sure?" She asked again. "I've been keeping an eye on him, but I can't be everywhere."

"I'm sure, Nelly." I smiled. It was refreshing that even though her little brother was now a legal adult, she still cared enough to call up his parole officer to make sure he was on the straight and narrow. "Somebody supervises the deposit now since he came in with the dog piss. It'd be kinda hard to sneak anything past Clyde."

"Is that the gay dude?" I could hear pots and pans clanking in the background. She cooked this boy three hot meals a day on top of raising her own two kids.

"You know what, you don't have to answer that." She said. And thank God. "It's unprofessional."

"It's all good." I adjusted the strap of my bag on my shoulder as I pulled the door open on my car then threw the bag into the front passenger seat. "And I'd love to chop it up but I gotta run."

"Oh, that's right. It's *All Black Everything* night. Is that lady gonna be there with the green bean jelly?"

It sounds disgusting but Miss Martha's Green Bean Jelly might be the best thing I've ever tasted. Especially on top of some fried chicken wings.

"She'll be there." I chuckled, climbing into the car and cranking it. "Y'all should come out. One of the vendors is doing free face-painting. Might be fun for the kids."

"Oh, we'll be there." She said. "I gotta restock on that jelly."

I said goodbye and ended the call, tired as hell and in need of a boost of energy before I arrived at the venue where me and my partner, Nick, hosted a bi-weekly market for black entrepreneurs in the Houston area. We'd been on it for the past three years now and I don't know how I found the strength to push through every other Friday after working sixty hours a week. But I did, and he did too. Guess you could say we were doing it for the culture. There was so much talent, original product, and just all-around excellence right under our noses. All that was needed was an avenue to bring it all forward. And that's where *ABE* came in.

"Wow! The crowd's grown since the last time I came out here." Jada exclaimed as we entered the main floor of a thriving weekly marketplace that she'd finally talked me into attending.

The smell of fried chicken, curry spices and incents had me feeling like I was levitating as I wheeled in my product, searching for a place for me and Jada to set up.

"This is absolute chaos," I said, eyes panning from one corner of the wide space covered in rectangular tables topped with various products from food to jewelry to beautiful black art.

From the exposed wood beams overhead to the mural of Kobe Bryant mounted on the stage that had to have been finished recently because I could still smell the paint, everything about this place screamed blackness and I couldn't wait to sink my teeth in.

"It is. And I love it!" Jada's eyes lit up as mine scrunched in anger because I still hadn't spotted a space to set up in this seemingly unorganized event.

"You're gonna sell out. I can feel it." She pressed her hands together before following my lead to the corner I'd called mine though it wasn't nearly spacious enough.

I don't think my sister understood how long it'd been since I'd left the house for anything other than bible study and playdates. I was completely out of my element and internally nervous as hell.

"I've been praying about it all week." I slanted my eyes at her, resting my palm on one of the two folded tables that would be holding my product once we found enough space to unfold them.

"That's good. But you won't need it." She said, running a hand over the customized salon chair that Daddy'd built for me that folded away just like the tables. "I doubt that there's another vendor in here doing beard balm massages."

"It's follicle rejuvenation. And I can't believe I let you talk me into bringing this thing." I rolled my eyes from her to the chair

"Sis, it's literally you massaging nigga's faces until they almost cum." She bucked her eyes while I kept on looking around for more space or somebody to come help me find the space I'd paid for.

"I don't know why you have to be so vulgar." I shook my head, propping a hand on my hip. "These are blessed products. Ain't nobody cummin'."

"Except Jared." She laughed through her nose.

"Jared hadn't been touched since the early nineties." I defended. "He probably came at the *thought* of cumming."

"True!" She laughed out loud. "But still…"

"You're trifling. You know that?" The search for space continued.

"Yep." She pursed her lips. "And that's exactly why you brought me."

I couldn't even debate her because she was absolutely right.

My head was down, searching my emails for contact information because there was no way I was gonna wander aimlessly around this warehouse looking for whoever was in charge. Finally, I located a number and a name at the bottom of a confirmation letter. I dialed the number with steam coming from my ears, prepared to curse whomever out in the name of the Lord.

"Hello." A deep voice answered, and I pulled the phone away from my ear to look at it because it caught me off guard.

"Yeah, this is… Angela Ford. I was calling to speak with the organizer of the ABE Market, Damien Briscoe."

"This is he. How can I help you?" He sounded like he was in the middle of a commotion similar to the one that I was standing in.

"You can, actually." I replied. "Especially since I paid you one hundred and fifty dollars for a spot that is apparently not available at your venue."

"I'm sorry. You said what?" His deep voice went up and octave under the steady chaos in his background.

"I *said*, I paid for a ten-by-ten space at the All Black Everything Market and have yet to locate that space after roaming around for the past ten minutes."

There was a pause over the phone that made me yell *"Hello?"* into the receiver. Meanwhile, Jada's attention had drifted off to the freckle-faced sister selling mood jewelry and yoga mats at a booth across from us.

"Yeah. I'm here. My bad." Now things sounded clearer on his end. Closer, even. "What side of the warehouse are you on?" He asked.

"To the left of the entry." I sighed, already frustrated with what was supposed to be a great experience. "And I doubt you'll be able to find space. So, a refund will be fine."

"I'm sorry, we don't issue refunds." He advised, verbally acknowledging someone that he must've been passing en route to wherever the hell he was heading.

"Excuse me?" I shrieked. "Either you can refund my money, or I can start a rough draft of the five-paragraph one-star review I plan on posting on your social media pages."

"Calm down." It sounded like he chuckled, but I knew I must've been hearing things. Because there was no way in hell a person was gonna take my money then laugh in my ear when I complained about their crappy ass customer service.

"Calm down? Did you just tell me to *calm down*? You have no idea how calm I am right now, sir. But you're about to find out."

"Girl, who are you going off on?" Jada's focus turned from the yoga mats to me.

"The organizer who overbooked this space and is currently on the phone talking to me like it's my damned fault."

"Who, Briscoe? Lemme see." Jada snatched the phone from my hand. Apparently, she knew the guy since working on *The Three Peas Morning Show* gave her access to every damn body.

"Wassup, Briscoe? My sister giving you problems?" She said with a smile on her face, hiking a brow at me.

Of course, I couldn't hear what he was saying on the other end, but I could tell by the smile sending Jada's cheekbones higher up that he was probably talking shit.

"It's okay. We'll see you when you get here." She nodded. "Okay. Okay, cool." She nodded some more before ending the call and handing me the phone.

"What's so funny? Is he a comedian too?" I accepted my phone from her hands.

"He kinda is." She trailed off a chuckle. "And he said he's gonna fix the problem. So, could you please *calm down?*"

"Funny." I rolled my eyes at her before looking down at my phone. "We've wasted twenty minutes already. We coulda been set up by now."

"But we're not. And nobody died." Jada nudged the side of me.

"Yet!" I bucked my eyes. "And where is he anyway? Are we supposed to just stand here indefinitely?"

"No. He's—"

"Hey, ladies. My bad." A tall, chocolate, thicker than necessary brother approached us, cutting right into whatever Jada was about to say and nearly pulling my eyes out of my head. "Busy day. No excuse."

"Hey, Briscoe!" Jada stepped up and pulled the big man into a hug. "It's all good. We don't have anything else planned for the night. And speaking of *we*, Angela, this is Briscoe. Briscoe, this is my extremely uptight and impatient sister, Penny."

"Nice to meet you, Penny." He extended for a handshake.

"It's *Angela*. And I wish I could say the same." I did not extend my hand, instead, folding my arms across my chest and shifting my weight to one hip.

"Alrighty then. Let's find you, ladies, a spot." Briscoe folded his full lips and took my response in stride, literally leading the way to a cramped spot between two food vendors, one selling cupcakes and the other cooking up Cajun cuisine. From where I was standing, it seemed like it'd be impossible for me to fit all of my things between all of theirs. But after brief discussions with each vendor, Briscoe not only helped them rearrange their things so that there was more than enough space, he also helped me and Jada unload our stuff.

"Is that okay?" He asked, having not said a word to me during the whole unloading process, which was more my fault than his.

"Nah, I think we're good," Jada replied for me because she knew my stubborn levels were almost consistently on ten.

"Alright." Briscoe nodded, shoving a pair of big hands in the pockets of his slacks before starting to back away, broad shoulders and muscled chest filling out a black T-Shirt with the event's name written across the front in bold white lettering. "If y'all need anything, just grab one of the staff members. They'll be wearing one of these." He tugged at the collar of his shirt.

"We will. Thanks, Briscoe." Jada offered a kind smile, getting straight to work unboxing product while I watched Briscoe walk away.

"He's fine, ain't he?" Jada's voice reminded me that I was supposed to be helping her instead of staring at the back of a man, being seduced by the thought of how strong he was, having just watched him lift a fifty-pound box of product like it was nothing but a jar of cotton balls.

"Huh?" I turned away from the view, secretly holding it in my mind for later.

"Huh, my ass. You heard me." She grinned. "That brother can fill out a pair of slacks. Got a strong back too."

"Fine or not, he could use some help in the organization department." I rounded the table to pull out display cases after Jada straightened the table covers.

"He fixed the problem, Penny. Give the man a break. It's always like this out here. I told you we should've left thirty minutes earlier."

"It's not my fault that Paul picked Boogie up late. And aside from that, we shouldn't have to be up here scrambling for good spots when we all paid the same buck. He needs to tape this shit off or something. Set some boundary lines. It's the professional thing to do."

"It's the professional thing to do." She mocked me. "You are so uptight, man."

"You say *uptight*, I say *paying customer*." I ripped the plastic off a stack of brochures and spread them out at the center of the table. "I wouldn't book two clients to share one chair. It's the same concept."

"Actually, the concept is you winning an argument and wanting to control every damn thing." She rolled her eyes.

"And? What's wrong with that?" I smirked.

"What's wrong is that you don't even know when you've won. The man not only made space for your mean ass, he stayed and helped us unload all this heavy shit. But you're so dead set on being right, that you can't accept an honest apology. *And* he's single, which doesn't really matter right now. But I'm just putting that out there."

I hated when Jada was right, and she knew I hated it when she was right. I hated it when anybody was right because it usually meant I was wrong.

"Fine." I could only use one word to accept defeat because it made my damn head hurt.

"Fine? Is that all you have?" Jada was gonna push it because she never knew when this miracle was gonna take place again.

"Fine. I'll give him a beard rejuvenation treatment and a free jar of balm. Is that good enough?" I looked to the side to find her filling the last of the sample cups with scented massage oils.

"Sounds perfect." She smiled without looking up at me. "Show the brother what them hands do. I see you, sis!"

"You don't see nothin'. Big-headed ass." I stuck my tongue out. Neatly gathering our empty boxes and storing them away under the table.

"Yeah. I love you too." She bumped my hip, giving me no choice but to shake my head and bump her back.

We'd survived the first hour and the crowd had evened out. The live band was up and running as a few patrons took to the dance floor. I'd made my rounds along with Nick, stopping by each table to make sure everybody was good. And toward the end of our tour, I received an offer for a complimentary beard rejuvenation treatment from the sister of a lady who could've sliced me smooth in half if looks could kill.

As with all of our vendors, the team did surface-level research before we approved vendor applications. It was a way to get a feel of their social media presence which in turn gave us an idea of what kind of crowd they'd be bringing with them. Angela Fold's following seemed to be booming. Mostly Christians with skin problems and lost souls in need of encouraging words from anyone attached to wealth and success. She was all about the spiritual quotes and typical things that people posted when they didn't want outsiders to know who they really were. And that was cool. Wasn't exactly my cup of tea, but I didn't knock her for doing what worked.

What surprised me most about Miss Fold was that although I didn't exactly connect to her online persona, there was something about her physical presence that spoke differently. There was an energy around her that was more felt than spoken. It jumped off of her chest and smashed right into me leaving me wondering if I'd imagined the whole thing. She held a sense of poise that was almost intimidating. And this is coming from a man who's not intimidated by shit. She demanded respect. Held folks accountable for their mistakes. And I respected that. It caught me off guard since it was our first time meeting. But it translated to her simply being a boss, obviously a necessary stance for a black, female entrepreneur.

Anyway, this was business. That energy shit didn't need to be entertained. I couldn't scare off a potential return vendor based on some tingles under my skin. I would, however, be taking my black ass over there to get my beard fondled. One hour into the market and almost all of the product was gone from her table and I hoped I hadn't missed out on whatever she was doing that had nigga's walking away glowing and shit.

"Briscoe, can I borrow you for a minute?" A loud voice sounded from behind me. I turned around to find Nelly standing at Miss Martha's Green Bean Jelly table, jumping up and down and waving her hand.

I looked toward Angela's table again and found that somebody else was already laid back in the chair getting their beard steamed. I smacked my lips and turned around in the opposite direction to see what the hell Nelly wanted.

"I'm so sorry. Were you busy?" Nelly asked, her youngest, Dexter, clinging to her leg.

"Nah. You're good. What's up?" I rustled a hand through Dexter's afro and he smiled like he always did, displaying a gap where his two front teeth used to be.

"I'm short," Nelly replied. "You got five bucks I can borrow? I'll send it with Dupre when he comes to see you next week."

"No worries. I got you." I nodded, reaching in my pocket and pulling out a crisp twenty.

"You sure? I don't like owing nobody money. Wouldn't want you to think you're paying for services or nothin'." She smacked her gum and gave me the same suggestive look she'd given me when I dropped Dupre off at her place one night.

"Never that." I grinned and shook my head, handing her the twenty, having no idea what she said next as I headed off toward Angela's table.

And then, "Briscoe!" The loud voice of my partner, Nick sounded from another end of the room. Was the universe working against me tonight? Was I ever gonna get this woman's hands on my face?

Luckily, I was tall enough to see over the top of the crowd and rushed over to see what the hell had Nick yelling. I made it to him just in time to find out he really didn't want shit.

"Hey, Briscoe." It was Shawndelle, the worst mistake I'd ever made in my whole damn life.

"Wassup, Shawn?" I tipped my chin at the short stack of crazy standing before me before mugging Nick for calling me across the room for this bullshit.

"Nothin'. I see y'all kept things up and running without me." Shawndelle propped a hand on what used to be a curvaceous hip, lips puckered and slathered with way too much lip gloss.

"Why wouldn't we? All you did was trash people's windshields with flyers at Walmart." Nick teased.

"Shut up." She rolled her eyes from Nick to me. "I'm sure Briscoe can tell you I did way more than that." She ran her tongue across her lips and not a single part of me reacted.

I didn't like the tone or suggestiveness in that statement. And if Shawndelle had brought her trifling ass all the way down from Austin, away from her new fiancé to try to spark something up with me, she was about to be sadly disappointed.

"Look, I got things to do." I looked down at her. "You need my help with something or did you just wanna show off your lip gloss?"

"Funny." She smirked while Nick laughed. "And you know you miss this lip gloss, nigga. Don't front."

"Does your fiancé know you're down here advertising expired goods?" She should've expected nothing but insults when she walked through the door.

"What fiancé?" That reply came so fast it had to be practiced. "We split. Turns out you were right." She held up an empty ring finger, probably expecting me to fall to my knees and beg her to step back into the spot that I'd occupied damn near three years ago.

"So, that's what this is?" I huffed. "You came way down here to let me know you're back on the market? Classy, Shawn. Real classy."

"What, you ain't interested? If memory serves me correctly, when I left, you were crying and shit. Begging for me to choose you. Did you forget all that?"

I hadn't forgotten any of it. But I also hadn't shared it with Nick or anybody else for that matter. Which is why I cut my eyes at the nigga signaling for him to walk off and mind his damn business.

"I'mma go get something to drink." Nick finally got the hint and went off toward the mobile bar vendor stationed a few tables down from Angela.

Angela.

Shit. The line was growing at her beard steaming chair. There was no way I was gonna get those hands on my face tonight.

"Briscoe?" Shawndelle's voice broke me out of a stare. That lime green dress Angela was wearing flowed over her slender curves like waves and I'd talked myself out of paying too much attention to it earlier because her attitude was stank.

"Yeah." I shook my head and looked down at her.

"Are you gonna answer me?"

"No," I replied.

"What do you mean no?"

"I mean *no*, I didn't forget that shit. And no, I don't feel the same way. And believe it or not, I'm sorry it didn't work out with old boy, but we could never be anything."

"Who is she?" She asked, lips curled with disappointment.

"Not that that's any of your business, but why does there have to be a she?" From the corner of my eye, I could see Angela gloving up, preparing to steam another beard. Niggas were falling asleep in the damn chair.

"Because what other reason would you have? Look at me." Shawndelle shifted her weight to one hip, and I couldn't help noticing how much weight the girl had lost.

"You know, it's funny that you're so worried about who I'm screwing when there's something far more important to be concerned about." I looked down into a set of eyes that used to make me think of honey but now didn't make me think of shit.

"Whatever." She threw up a hand.

"Yeah, whatever." I returned. "If there's nothing else…"

"Actually, there…there is." Her tone softened and she started twiddling her fingers, a direct indication that she was about to ask for something that I didn't have or wouldn't wanna give.

"Shawn, if you're about to ask me for money—"

"I'm not." She interrupted, looking up from her hands. "I do need a favor though."

"What is it?" I don't know why I asked. I'd extended enough favors to this woman to build a bridge from Houston to China.

"It's just… You know I left everything when I moved to Austin." She said.

"Yeah. I was one of the things."

"And I'm sorry about that. I really am. But I just…I don't have anywhere to go. And I was wondering if maybe—"

"Hell no!" I almost yelled.

The fucking audacity.

"Briscoe, please? Just until I get back on my feet. You know I got hustle. Thirty days tops and I'm outta your hair."

"Are you smokin'?" I had to ask. She had to be on drugs to think that I was gonna have her living under my roof after she ran off on me with a nigga without so much as a fuck you, good-bye.

"Look, I know I did you dirty, okay. And I can't undo that. I fucked up."

"Yeah, you did. And you don't get a chance to fuck up again. What happened to all your friends? The ones that helped you gas up my car and drive down there to that nigga? They ain't got a couch you can crash on til the next nigga comes along?"

"I deserve that." She kept her voice light and friendly. It was all a part of the game played by a master fucking manipulator. "And I also deserve to have lost contact with those friends when Alonso convinced me that he was all I needed."

I shrugged and said, "Man, I don't know what you expect me to do with all that." It wasn't like me to be cold to anybody, especially not when they were down on their luck. But all this shit was her fault. She needed to blame karma, not me.

"I just need a month. Thirty days tops and you can be rid of me for good. Trust me, if I had anybody else to go to I would. I know you hate me. You have every right to."

"I don't hate nobody." I sighed, half of me ready to send her on her homeless ass way, the other half speaking to me in my mother's voice about forgiveness and all the other things that Jesus would do.

"Thirty days." I decided before the Devil resurfaced on my right shoulder. "And we need to establish some house rules before you walk through the door, so we might as well head out and discuss 'em now."

"Okay." I'd never seen her so docile. Guess desperate times called for desperate measures.

"Damien." My mother was one of a handful of people who called me by my first name.

"I know." I walked through the door of her apartment, the smell of bleach and Pine-Sol taking over where the smell of dinner had disappeared before I showed up.

"But do you?"

"Yes. And I already know what you're thinking. But it's not like that. The whole situation is temporary."

"*Temporary* is the problem." She stepped back as I walked in, full figure stopping just beyond the doorway to look up into the eyes of her one and only child. "You think that's good enough? You think this is some machine you can turn off then turn back on without anybody being affected? How many times, Damien? How many times are we gonna go through this before it's enough? She couldn't even come in here to speak."

"Ma, I need you to calm down." I reached over and took her plump hands into mine. "And she didn't come in because the last time she did you tried to douse her with holy water. I got this, alright? You don't need to keep stressing about everything. You're gonna run your blood pressure up."

"No, *you're* gonna run my blood pressure up." She kept on fussing as I ushered her over to the sofa. "Every time it's something else. She's a manipulator and you know she is. And who's the one who suffers? Huh? Who's the one she hurts the most in all this?"

"Daddy!" The squeaky voice of my favorite person in the world sounded from down the hallway, followed by him running full speed into me and roping his arms around my waist.

"Wassup, man?" I leaned over to pick up the fifty-pound five-year-old who looked more like me than I did.

"Nothin'." He looked me right in the eyes and smiled. "Did you bring me something from the market?" Dude was always putting the beg on.

"Is that how you do me? No *'I love you, Daddy'*? *'I missed you, Daddy'*? Just straight to the goods, huh?" I tickled his belly and he curled against me giggling like he always did.

"You know I love you, man!" He said through a chuckle, hugging my neck tight then leaning back to see if I had anything.

"That's more like it." I poked his belly again. "And I got you something in the car. Go get your backpack."

"Yes!" He extended a fist then pulled it in as I lowered him to the floor to go grab his things.

And as soon as he was out of earshot, I knew Mama was about to say something.

"You see that?" She slanted her eyes up at me from her seat on the sofa. "That's a happy child. And you're about to wash all that away because that trifling mother of his came running back with a sob story."

"You know Mama, I expected you of all people to be more compassionate." I glanced down the hallway to make sure DJ wasn't coming. "The only reason I even said yes to this was because your voice was in my head saying I should."

"Oh, baby that wasn't my voice." Her eyes widened as she grabbed the remote and flipped on the TV. "My voice would've told you to pray and send her on her way."

"Ma!?"

"I'm serious." She huffed, settling into her seat and navigating through the search menu like DJ had taught her. "Every problem ain't yours to solve. And you have more to consider than getting stiffed on the rent."

"I'm not charging her."

"Then you're crazier than I thought." She shook her head. "Lost a whole car behind this woman. Her sugar bowl must be made of gold."

"You know what…"

"I'm ready, Daddy. Let's go get my gift!" DJ came back just in the nick of time.

"And where do you think you're going without giving me a kiss?" Mama looked over at her spoiled rotten grandson and planted a palm on her knee.

"Sorry, Momma." He hurried over and ran into her outreached arms, planting a kiss on her cheek. "I love you." He said before she released him.

"And I love you too, baby." Mama smiled before slanting her eyes up at me. "More than anything in this world." She said with emphasis. And all I could do was sigh.

"I'll see you in the morning." I leaned in to kiss her cheek.

"I'll be here." She rolled her eyes with nothing but judgment painting her round brown face. I was never gonna hear the end of this shit. I knew that before I decided to be the good Samaritan.

"I think somebody's in your car, Daddy. You better call the police."

The kid noticed everything because he was nosey like his grandma.

"We're good, man." I rubbed my hand over his fade. "There's something I need to tell you before we get to the car, though. Some big boy stuff." I squatted down so that we were face to face, a subtle breeze brushing past us that I'd hoped was carrying some kind of calming agent.

The last time DJ had seen his mother, he was only two years old. I didn't know if he'd notice her face outside of the pictures framed in his room.

"Is this about me covering my hands with glue in Miss Huerta's class? I promise I won't do it again." His little voice was loaded with worry.

I chuckled. "Nah, man. You're good." I brushed my hands down the sides of his arms. "But you're right, there is somebody in my car."

"Who?" He leaned to the side and tried to look past me.

"It's Shawndelle." I didn't hesitate. There was no room for it. I was raising my boy to be upfront and to the point about things. No waiting for emotions to lead the way. Just put it out there when it's honest and true.

"You mean my mama, Shawndelle?" He asked to be sure, I guess.

"Yeah." I nodded, keeping my eyes on his, watching as his little fingers locked together in front of him. "I know this is gonna be a little bit different for you, man. But she's gonna be staying with us for a while. Not for good, just for a little while."

"Where's she gonna sleep?" I didn't have a guide on which questions would be on this exam, but I guess I should've seen that one coming.

"In the guest room."

"That's close to my room." His eyes went wide.

"Yeah. Yeah, it is. Are you okay with that? 'Cause if you're not…"

"It's ok, I guess." He shrugged his shoulders. "Can we go home now? I'm sleepy." He yawned, looking into my eyes.

"Yeah. We can go. You sure you're okay with all this?"

"I'm sure, Daddy." He said before I kissed him on the forehead and pulled him against my chest for a hug. I had a feeling I was making a big mistake but didn't know what other choice I had.

"Hi," DJ spoke first as soon as I opened the car door because I'd always taught him that the one entering the space should be the first one to speak.

"Oh, hey!" Shawndelle looked up from her phone. She'd probably just wrapped up selfie session, not at all preparing for the enormity of this situation. "You got so big!" She looked over her shoulder at DJ instead of getting out of the damn car and rushing back there to hug him like any mother who hadn't seen in their child in two years would.

"Say cheese!"

"Don't. Don't say cheese, DJ." I put a hand in front of her phone and cut my eyes at her. "Put your seatbelt on, son." I looked back at my son.

"But I just—"

"Don't." I cut her off. "This ain't that. Just… chill, alright?"

"Fine." She rolled her eyes and sat back in her seat. God, I should've just let her sleep under a damn bridge. I was gonna have to reprogram my son in four damn weeks.

"Is it cold in Austin?" DJ asked as soon as I cranked the car. "My friend Lori said she went one time for Christmas break and the roads had ice on 'em."

"Yeah, it's…it's cold sometimes, I guess." Shawndelle entertained, looking back at him. "You know what else is special about Austin? It's the state capital of Texas." I was surprised she knew seeing as geography facts didn't come with a check attached.

"I know," DJ said. "I know all the state capitals. Daddy taught me. And I can spell 'em too. You wanna see?" He reached into his backpack and pulled out the newest journal he'd been filling up with random information that he found on the internet during after school discovery time with Mama."

"D, it's late. I'm sure she doesn't wanna see all that. Maybe tomorrow." I swooped in to save her from being bored to death by shit that she didn't care about.

"What? Of course, I wanna see. Show me." She smiled and so did he. And I couldn't wait to get to the house and go off about this shit.

The next fifteen minutes were filled with DJ showing off his skills and Shawndelle pretending to care. And from the outside looking in this whole scene was made for TV. Fortunately, I knew better. She didn't want our son when she was pregnant and sure as hell didn't want him now. I literally had to beg her to keep him. And the minute she saw an escape route from motherhood, she took it and didn't look back.

Until now.

Now that she'd been dropped on her ass and needed a way out, she was here, willing to show some fake love until the next shiny thing passed by. And I knew this. Could see her schemes from a mile away. It was my responsibility to protect my son and I'd do that at all costs.

"Kill that shit, Shawn," I said after tucking DJ into bed. "And don't act like you don't know what I'm talking about because I know damn well you do."

"But he's here, Briscoe. What am I supposed to do, ignore him?" She gripped the handle on her luggage and stood beside the couch in my living room.

"That's what you've been doing for the past two years so it wouldn't be much of a stretch." I walked past her into the kitchen to grab a bottled water. "I don't expect you to be cold to him while you're under the same roof. But at the same time, I don't need you giving him false hope."

"False hope? What the hell is that supposed to mean?" She turned around and darted her eyes to the kitchen.

"It means you can drop the whole, *I wanna get to know you'*, skit. He's already used to you not being around. He's in a good place and I don't need you fucking that up."

"So, what, you want me to play deaf when he asks me questions? You got some kind of magic potion that can make me invisible until he heads off to school in the morning?"

I downed the rest of the water and dropped the empty bottle in the trash can, all while she watched in suspense waiting for me to respond. "That'd be perfect. But since it's not possible, you can just stick to keeping a low profile. And I hate to be a shitty host, but I've had a long day. You know where everything is. Good night."

I brushed past her in route to my bedroom, barely fazed by the look of sadness in her eyes because the shit was as fake as the weave hanging down her back. I peeped in on DJ to find that he was sound asleep and then I went into my room and slammed the door behind me, opening the calendar on my phone and starting a thirty-day countdown ending on the day that I'd be sending this woman on her way.

Five

It was the same building where I'd learned my ABC's. The same cafeteria where I'd learned how to open a carton of milk all by myself, refusing the teacher's help because Mama'd told me I was a big girl. The tables and chairs were so small that I couldn't imagine I'd ever fit into one. Yet here I was, dropping my own little person off to take up a tiny seat at a tiny table on her first day at Kids First Head Start.

"Are you sure you don't want Mommy to stay a little longer?" I asked Patience, fixing the bright pink bow in her hair for the one-hundredth time and likely getting on her nerves. "I don't mind. I know this is a little scary."

"Mommy, look We have a library!" She hadn't heard a word I said. Her little eyes were taking in all the colors and centers spanning from one end of the classroom to the other.

"I see that. You want me to stay and help you find a book?" That request was more for me than her. Ever since the day I was well enough to come out of postpartum depression, I'd been going headfirst into making sure that Patience knew she was the very center of my joy.

"No, thank you, Mommy. I can do it by myself. I'm a big girl, remember?" I'd been telling her that all summer in preparation for the coming school year. Turns out I'd convinced her but failed to convince myself.

"Yes, you are, baby." I swallowed the lump in my throat, and she must've noticed the shakiness in my voice.

"It's gonna be okay, Mommy. We can get some ice cream when you pick me up at two." She rubbed her tiny hand down the side of my face, and it was all I could do not to break down on that floor, sitting Indian style in a pair of blue jeans because I'd already made plans to spend the day at her school.

"You okay, mom?" Patience's teacher, Miss Stidham came over to check on me. I must've looked pitiful being comforted by my four-year-old daughter.

"Yes, I'm…I'm okay." I cleared my throat, kissing Patience's hand before I got up off the floor. "It's just harder than I expected."

"It's okay." Miss Stidham smiled, Senegalese twists pulled up into a bun on top of her head. "The first day is always the hardest. But you can rest assured that Patience is in good hands." She rubbed a hand over my baby's shoulder, and Patience smiled up at her then directed her smile to me. And in that instant, I knew that if I didn't get out of there, I was gonna break down into uncontrollable sobbing.

"Ok," I said, running a thumb down Patience's cheek. "I love you, Boogie. Do you know how much?"

"This wide." She stretched her little arms as far as they'd go. "And this high!" She jumped as high as she could before I leaned over, planted a kiss on her cheek and hurried out of the classroom as I felt the damn breaking behind my eyes.

"First-day blues?"

I recognized the voice but had to clear the tears from my eyes to see who it was.

"Just dropped mine off too." He continued before I could reply. "Can't get to the car fast enough. It's year two and the first day is still hard."

When my eyes cleared, I recognized who he was and was stuck between asking why he was talking to me and asking if he wanted to go somewhere and talk a little more.

"My bad, you probably don't remember me."

"Damien." I interrupted. "How could I forget the man who parted a sea of food vendors to make space for me?"

"Ok, so you *do* remember?" He smiled, barely. His face was almost completely void of smile lines which meant he was either mean as hell or didn't have much to smile about.

"I do," I said, feeling awkward as hell standing in the middle of the hallway, completely shadowed by the massiveness of his body. "You said you have a kid here?"

"Yeah. DJ, my son. I guess you could say he's a senior." There went that half-smile again. I'd decided that the mention of his son might be the one thing to bring it about.

"If you don't mind my asking, how's it been for him here? I mean, I went when I was little but that's not much of a reference point so many years later."

"How many years?"

"Excuse me?"

"Since you've been here? How long?"

"You know what, you could teach a class on what *not* to say to a lady." I tried to act offended but the fact that I was still standing there clearly sent the opposite message.

"I got a better idea." He shoved his hands into the pockets of a pair of black slacks that conformed to his thick legs with tailored perfection. "There's a coffee shop right across the street. Why don't you join me? Maybe gimme some pointers on what I *should* say."

This was game and I knew it because the game never changed.

Profile a sister.

Push her buttons and all that shit.

Reel her in with seemingly innocent propositions to break down her defenses.

Get in her pants.

Ruin her life.

Lather.

Rinse.

Repeat.

Luckily for him, I'd taken the day off to stalk my daughter. I had time to play and I'd be doing just that. My radar was too sensitive to ever be played or played *with* again. The most he'd be getting from me was some surface-level convo with a few packages of sugar and cream.

"Sure." I looked up into a set of eyes that were as dark as the tapered box covering the top of his head.

"Cool." He nodded. "We can use the crosswalk if you don't mind. It's hell getting outta this parking lot with all the first-timers coming in."

She wore a pale pink cashmere sweater with high heeled booties to match, and dark blue jeans that made her look softer and approachable. Short, kinky coils framed her pretty brown face with cheekbones so high it looked like she was smiling even when she wasn't. A barely detectible scent floated around her like a barrier, softly whispering and reminding me of exactly who she was.

She waited without looking back at me as we approached the door to the coffee shop. It must've been second nature to have folks at her beck and call. Luckily, I was a gentleman. It didn't take a second for me to pull the door open. And it was a good thing mom and pops had raised me right because the only thing better than Angela from the front was definitely Angela from behind.

An ample behind rounded her slender frame, heels forcing the perfect posture and that arch in her back. She couldn't have known how enticing she was by design. How damn near impossible it was to concentrate on anything else in her presence. If she did, she wouldn't step foot out of the house, not without covering herself from head to toe in prayer cloths and choir robes.

"So, what're you having? My treat." She looked up at the menu as we stood behind the next person in line.

"Nah, I got it." I looked down my arm, eyes landing on her neck and even that shit was sexy. "I'll have a tall pecan blend, black," I said when asked by the cashier. "And the lady will have the same with a shot of vanilla and three creams."

"But I—"

"Trust me." I winked. "I wouldn't steer you wrong."

She accepted my proposal. Both proposals, actually. And that set the course of a morning that I didn't see coming. After receiving our drinks, we took seats near the window at a table for two with the sun casting a glow over the space that I could've very well been imagining. I took a sip from my coffee, indulging in the bold taste that perfectly matched the coffee's aroma. Then I waited for the verdict as Angela put her cup to her lips and blew before carefully taking the first sip.

"Wow!" Her eyes widened, focusing on everything and nothing at the same time.

"Wow, *it's good as hell* or wow *you wanna pour it in the toilet*?" I asked though the smile on her face answered the question for me.

"Good as hell for a thousand, Alex!" She laughed, and for reasons that I could barely comprehend, I felt accomplished as hell for making that happen.

"I never would've picked this. Thank you." She put up a hand and said after taking another, longer sip.

"Lemme guess. You're more of a house blend sugar and cream kinda girl?" I teased, putting my drink down on the table.

"Either you've been peeping through my kitchen window or you're some kind of coffee psychic." She said, placing her coffee on the table after a third sip.

"Coffee psychic?" I teasingly squinted.

"I said what I said." She smirked, full lips curving to the side.

"Aight." I bowed my head in defeat. "Guess I'll be that."

"Yes, you will." She chuckled; a soft yet throaty sound that felt like a prize.

From the corner of my eye, I could see her observing me, taking me in without flinching as I pulled my drink to my lips. Under any other circumstances, I might've asked if something was wrong. But with Angela, I didn't mind. Might even say I wanted her to keep on looking.

"So, Damien, what do you do when you're not guessing people's coffee preferences?" She seamlessly transitioned from staring to ask.

"I'm a probation officer," I replied. "And you can call me Briscoe."

"Is that what you prefer? Cause I kinda like Damien." I didn't see that coming and sure as hell wasn't prepared to respond.

"I mean it's… it doesn't really matter, I guess." I shrugged. "I'm just used to being called Briscoe."

"Then you can get *used* to being called Damien. I mean, for the duration of this…"

"This what?" I grinned because she looked nervous as hell and that didn't at all fit her personality.

"This…coffee reading." I had to give her eight out of ten on the wit scale.

"Alright." I nodded. "And what do you do when you're not threatening to leave one-star reviews, steaming beards and convincing people that they can't live without your shea butter?"

"That's funny." She slanted her eyes at me before taking a sip from her coffee. "You're a natural-born comedian, you know that?"

"Well, I have been responsible for a chuckle or two."

"Or two?"

"It's my average."

"Hilarious!" She threw her head back, exaggerating, unintentionally drawing my attention back to that long neck.

"Anyway," She cleared her throat. "I own a full-service spa."

"Really? Did you have cards at the market? I must've missed that detail."

"No. You didn't miss it." She replied. "*The Hem* is a different entity. I don't usually cross-promote it with my handmade products."

"Shit, why not? That stuff was flying off the tables." I looked at her sideways.

"I know!" She giggled. "We do pretty good numbers online, too. But all those proceeds go to my nonprofit. It's helped to keep us afloat for the past ten years."

"Wow, a nonprofit too? I see you Super Woman!" I teased.

"Stop!" She flipped a hand. "Nothing super about it. Just doing what the Lord called me to do."

"I feel you." I nodded, cellphone vibrating in my pocket reminding me that my ass needed to get to work. "I'm so sorry, I gotta get outta here before they bust my door down," I said, pulling my phone from my pocket looking at the time and realizing I had less than thirty minutes to get to the office.

"Oh. No, it's okay." She said, pushing back from the table, waiting for me to stand before she did the same. "It was nice talking with you, Damien." She said my name like she enjoyed it.

"It was nice talking with you too, Angela," I replied. And it was no surprise that I enjoyed saying her name too.

We left the coffee shop, trotting through the crosswalk taking advantage of the crawling speed from the last of the school zone traffic. As we approached her car, I mustered up the strength to swallow my pride and shoot my shot. Because what were the chances that we'd be in the same space again? How could I ignore the fact that the universe had placed us in the same hallway?

"So, I was wondering if… maybe could do this again sometime?" It sounded so much smoother in my head. I was way off my damn game.

"I don't know." She said, confusing me. "Is that how psychic coffee readings work? I mean you know so much more about me now it hardly seems fair."

Oh, so she was teasing me. I'd take that as a good sign. It was better than a hell no which was exactly what I'd expected.

"I'll be here every morning for at least the next two weeks because I'm a hover mother and I can't help myself." She hit the remote on her car keys and I reached past her to pull the door open.

"Then I guess I'll be here too." I looked down into her eyes, accepting a reciprocal gaze of curiosity that blended with the soft scent I'd decided was simply *her* and not some concoction from a jar

Six

It's amazing the things you could learn about a person over coffee. All their pet-peeves and subtle mannerisms. Even their relationship with God or the lack thereof rose up like steam from a cup of pecan blend under the right circumstances. I had to give it to him, Damien was good at covering his hand. But I saw right through it. Wouldn't dare be hypnotized by a full set of lips and shoulders broad enough to carry the weight of the world without missing a step. I had a spirit to protect at all costs and had successfully done so for the past two weeks.

But I'll be damned if it wasn't getting harder by the minute. I was going into the prayer closet three times a day just to ward off the weakness of my flesh.

"So, what're you doing tonight? Rubbing one out?" Jada's vulgarity was bound to set her hair on fire one day, sitting across the table from me as we had lunch a few blocks up from the spa.

"No, freak." I stabbed my fork into her salad, stealing a cherry tomato since I'd eaten all of mine. "Patience is with Paul for the weekend and I'm gonna enjoy some peace and quiet."

"Sounds boring." She rolled her eyes.

"That's because you're not somebody's mama," I noted. "I love my baby, but she's a full-time job. Do you know they send her home with homework? *Homework*, Jada. She's four."

"I'm not surprised." She shook her head. "The most we had to worry about at her age was how many crayons we could stuff up our noses."

"Nah, that was you and Chad." I forked a leaf of lettuce into my mouth. "Y'all were touched and not in a good way."

"You know what, fuck you." She flicked a sliced almond, hitting me in the nose.

"Truth hurts, kid." I wiped the almond off my nose with a napkin and took a sip from my sweet tea.

"Whatever." She took a sip from her drink. "Anyway, what's up with you and Briscoe? Y'all still drinking *nigga nut coffee* and pretending you don't wanna see what's under each other's clothes?"

"It's *'pecan blend'* and this is why I never tell you anything." I dropped my napkin on the table, offering a kind smile to the waitress when she placed our ticket on the table. "Your mind is always in the gutter."

"Because the gutter is a nice place. Matter of fact, I don't think it should even be called a gutter anymore."

With Jada, it would've been safer not to entertain the thought. But because I was apparently a glutton for punishment, I asked: "What name do you suggest, Jada?"

"The Broom Closet." She said without missing a beat. This was exactly why she was the perfect fit for a morning radio show.

"I'm not gonna ask why but I know you're gonna tell me anyway." I slipped the bill and a tip in the black leather folder and pushed it to the edge of the table.

"It's simple." She said, making all kinds of noise as she reached the bottom of her drink and refused to stop sucking until there was nothing left but ice. "Broom closets hold all kinds of useful things. I have never walked into a broom closet without coming out with exactly what I went in for."

"You're a sick person, you know that?" I shook my head at my crazy as hell little sister.

"Judge me all you want. But you and I both know that your ass needs a trip to the *Broom Closet*. How long has it been?"

"I'm not entertaining that question and I need to get back to work where people actually have good sense."

"Wow, that long, huh!?" Her eyes went wide as we both stood from the table, the only similarity between us being the shape of our eyes, lips, and hips.

"I don't record my orgasms, you pervert." I defended because it had been forever since I'd had one.

"And if you did, you'd have to knock three inches of dust off the record book." She bumped my hip and laughed as we walked out of the door.

"Forget you." I elbowed her before allowing her to pull me into a side hug.

"You know I love you, girl." She kissed me on the cheek.

"And I love you too, freak." I kissed her cheek before we hurried off to our vehicles to go on with the rest of our day.

"Who left this?" I walked back into *The Hem* to find a huge bouquet of peach-colored roses on my desk.

Our receptionist, Ms. Davie, could hardly contain herself long enough to let me make it back there to them. And when I did, she exploded into giggles with a smile on her face as wide as the sky.

"What are you smiling at?" I asked, confusion folding my lips as I plucked a peach card that matched the flowers from a thick plastic cardholder tucked into the glass vase.

"Because those flowers are beautiful, and you deserve flowers, and I can't wait to meet whoever sent them because God knows it's taken long enough!" She rattled off without taking a breath in between because rattling was Ms. Davie's only mode of communication.

"First of all, you are way too invested in my personal life." I eased down into the comfy chair behind my desk. "And second, this is probably just a thank you gift for the community outreach ministries."

"Yeah, I doubt it." She took a seat across from me and crossed one chubby leg over the other. "Roses are a symbol of love or the desire to have it, honey, and I doubt the kids at The Bricks are sending that kind of message."

"Ms. Davie—"

"You know I'm right." She cut me off, shaking her foot with anticipation. "Now open that card so I can live vicariously through you."

Those plump cheeks were already raising again, and I hadn't even opened the card. A head full of gray candy curls falling over her bouncing shoulders reminded me that she was thirty years my senior.

"And why do you have to live through me, Ms. Davie? You could still snag a husband if you wanted to." I teased since she was always teasing me.

"Girl, the last thing I want, or need is a husband." She said. "An *'in and out'*, maybe. But after being married and divorced three times, a husband ain't even in the top ten on my list of needs."

"I'm scared to ask, but what exactly is an *'in and out'*?" I looked down at the card and peeled the envelope open.

"It's self-explanatory, honey." She slanted her eyes. "Come in, take care of business, and then get out." She ended with a nod, certain that I was a grown enough woman to get her drift.

And I did. Laughing so hard I had to compose myself to finish opening the card. And when I did, my eyes went straight to the bottom instead of reading from the top like a normal human being.

"Well, who's it from?" Ms. Davie was nearly coming unglued.

"Nobody," I replied because it was easier than telling the truth.

"Well if *nobody* makes you smile like that, I'd love to see what *somebody* could do." She smirked.

"It's from a friend," I said. "Kind of..."

"Girl, is it a friend or not? You young people sure know how to make mountains out of molehills."

"It's...kinda complicated."

"I bet it's not."

"But it is."

"Try me." Ms. Davie's big eyes bucked as she leaned back in the chair folding her arms across her ample chest.

I sighed, "It's just a guy I've been having coffee with every morning for the past couple of weeks. His son goes to the same school as Patience. It's no big deal, really."

"Oh, I see." She nodded her head as if she'd heard something that I didn't say out loud.

"You see what?" I looked up from the card having read nothing more than Damien's name at the bottom.

"What you *can't* see, apparently." She slid forward in the chair then stood up as the door chimed at the front of the spa. "If he was okay with continuing these coffee conversations without the promise of anything else, you wouldn't be sitting in front of two dozen roses holding that card in your hand like it had a million-dollar check attached to it. If that's an invitation to any place but a coffee shop, I'd advise you to go. You're too young and too beautiful and definitely too smart to pass on the opportunity to be loved the right way."

Ms. Davie dropped that jewel then swished her wide hips out of my office, greeting whoever was standing at the counter like it was all in a day's work.

Unknown: The flowers are beautiful.

The text came from an unknown number, but I'd only sent flowers to one woman, so it wasn't that hard to figure out. I still had to give her a hard time though. After two solid weeks of sitting two feet across from each other, I still didn't have her number. Well, that is until now since I'd left mine in the card attached to her roses.

Me: Who is this?

A week ago, I would've regretted sending that text because Angela seemed so serious. But a few layers had been peeled back during our forty-five-minute chats. She was still guarded as hell, but not nearly as much as day one.

Unknown: Funny!

Obviously, I couldn't see her face, but I can guarantee she was smiling.

Me: It's what I do! And since you got my number, I'm assuming you read the rest of the card?

Unknown: That would be a false assumption…

Great. This was just great. Thought I'd cut myself some slack by asking her out with a card, but I should've known that nothing would be that easy with Angela.

Me: Cool. You still at the office?

It wasn't like I was afraid to ask a woman out.

Unknown: Yep. Why? Are you trying to make an appointment?

Me: Actually, I was hoping you'd take me as a walk-in.

Unknown: That can be arranged. How soon? My next client's not due 'til 3 pm.

Me: Aight. I'm omw.

I prayed she didn't think I was a creep for being available on such short notice. But it just so happened that I was on her side of town. The Lord works in mysterious ways.

I'd gifted spa days to my mama and aunts more times than I could count on my fingers and toes. But I'd never stepped into one to treat myself, and definitely had never seen one laid out like *The Hem*. Mint green walls rose from blond wood floors and wide windows were frosted with *The Hem* in clear lettering like someone had traced their finger through the frost on the windows. Soft music played overhead and the smell in this place was heavenly. It felt fluid, for lack of better words. From the reclining seats in the waiting area to the round receptionist desk. Everything about this place begged you to walk in farther. And although I only had an hour to burn, that's exactly what I intended to do.

"Hello, sir. Welcome to The Hem. How can I help you today?" A short, round woman sitting behind the front desk asked, pulling my eyes away from the fifty-inch screen mounted on the wall in the waiting area.

"How're you doin', ma'am." I offered a polite smile that was probably barely detectable because I didn't smile much. "I'm here to see Angela. Said she'd take me as a walk-in."

"Ooooohhh…" The lady put a plump hand to her chest, round cheeks rising beneath a set of light brown eyes. "You wouldn't happen to be the man responsible for those beautiful roses on her desk, now would you?"

Damn. That was a bold assumption.

"I, um…"

"Hello, Damien." Angela came from around the corner just in the nick of time. "I apologize if Ms. Davie is up here harassing you. It's kind of what she does." She cut her eyes at Ms. Davie and all she could do was smile and shrug.

"Come on back." Angela headed off toward the area she'd just emerged from, slender hips swaying, unintentionally drawing my attention while Ms. Davie watched me try my damndest not to react, still smiling hard as hell.

He had no business walking into my establishment looking and smelling this good, and I had no business inviting him. But here we were, centimeters apart as he laid back in the steaming chair trusting me to do whatever I was about to do.

I'd already prepped his beard and skin with a hypoallergenic wipe, spending the whole three minutes fighting the urge to trace my finger over his lips to see if they were as soft as they looked. It was a good thing Damien didn't smile much. Seeing any kind of reaction on his face in response to me touching him at all might have had me acting very unprofessional, running off to the restroom to gather myself.

"So, what has you on this side of town?" I asked, stepping away for a moment to grab the beard balm from the warming bowl.

"A client." He replied, turning his head to the side to look at me from across the room. "You'd be surprised how many folks in The Woodlands are on probation."

"I bet I wouldn't." I giggled. "More money, more problems, right?" I picked up the warmed balm and walked back over to

Damien, taking in the fullness of his shoulders under the mint green smock that I'd draped over him to protect his clothing.

"Gospel truth." He hiked his brows before letting his eyes fall closed as I ran a palm over his beard.

It was already so soft, he really didn't need a treatment. But I wouldn't dare say that out loud.

"Speaking of the gospel, what church do you belong to?" I couldn't believe that hadn't come up in conversation. But there was something about that moment, literally having him in my hands that made me wanna know more about his familiarity with the house of the Lord.

"I don't belong to a church." He answered with his eyes still closed.

"Oh." Was my response because I didn't know what else to say.

"Oh, *that's a shame*, or oh *that' ok*?" Now his eyes were open and slanted up at me as I took my hand from his beard to dip it in the warm balm.

"Neither." I shrugged. "It was just a question and you answered it." I rubbed the balm briskly between my palms before working it through the soft, silky hairs of his beard.

He didn't close his eyes this time which I'll admit, had me a little unnerved. The way he stared at me like he knew I had more to say but wouldn't dare say it. Like he was actually reading my mind.

"But are you pleased with the answer?" He spoke with my fingertips massaging the flesh of his chin.

"Of course, I'm not pleased with the answer, Damien. I'm a Christian. I want everybody to go to church." That was always my thought when people said they didn't go to church, but I'd never ever been brave enough to say it out loud.

"I'm not judging you, it's…"

"You don't have to explain yourself." He cut me off, eyes falling closed as I massaged my way up the sides of his face. "I just wanted you to be honest."

"Do you think I'm not an honest person?" I spread both thumbs across his forehead, just below the crisp edge of his hairline.

"No." He almost whispered. The facial was taking the bass out of his voice. "I just think you hold back on certain things and do the opposite on others."

"And what's wrong with that? Everybody doesn't need to know everything that's going on in my head."

"But I'm not everybody." He opened his eyes. "Or am I?" He looked up at me as I smoothed the shea butter exfoliator down the slope of his nose.

"Damien."

"Angela?"

"I don't know what you're tryna do here. But I—"

"Come out with me tonight." He cut me off again. And it was hard to get upset about that with his long legs stretching the entire length of my steaming chair.

"I tried asking you with a card but apparently you only read names and numbers." He smiled…barely.

"I read the card," I admitted. "And it's really nice of you. I'm flattered, seriously. But I—"

"Have nothing planned and a whole weekend to yourself because your daughter's with her father. You told me so over coffee this morning."

God, I asked you for a man who listens and now one was lying in my chair. You do have a sense of humor.

"So?" He pressed.

"So, what?" I played dumb, snatching two wipes from the dispenser and cleaning off his face.

"We on or you scared?" He laid his head back, already celebrating my response before it even left my lips.

"Fine." I rolled my eyes and shook my head. "Put this on and shut up." I handed him a satin eye cover, then powered on the steamer, blowing a signature skin treatment over his beautiful bronze skin, standing in disbelief of what I'd just agreed to.

Seven

"Well, don't you look dapper?" Mama opened the door and took DJ's hand. I already knew she was about to gas me up. It had been a minute since she'd seen me dressed for anything but work.

"Thanks." I played it modestly because I hated being under the spotlight.

"Daddy got a date!" DJ was more excited than me. From the minute I told him why he'd be spending the night at Mama's, he'd been firing off questions one after another.

"I heard." Mama squeaked as he snatched his backpack from my hand and dropped it on the sofa. "They're going dancing at Poppa's place." He rattled off, pulling pajamas from his bag, excited to take a bath in Mama's bathtub because she had jacuzzi jets that made more bubbles than he needed.

"Wait, you're taking this woman to the Sugar Shack? Damien…"

"Ma, don't start man." I dropped my head to the side, mean-mugging my son because that was supposed to be our secret.

"I'm not startin'." She put up a hand and turned to walk into the kitchen. "I'm just sayin…"

"Well, don't just say." I cut in, following her to the kitchen and leaning on the island while she pulled DJ's snacks from the frig. "I know it's not the ideal spot for a first date, but I don't want things to be too formal. She's a little uptight. I just wanna see her let her hair down and have a good time."

"So, you're trying to change her already? How long have you known this woman?"

"Not long. And I'm not tryna change her." I defended because I wasn't. "I like the way she is. Just feels like she's holding a lot in."

"And you think taking her to your father's hole in the wall night club is gonna pull things out? Have I taught you nothing in thirty-six years?" She shook her head, popping a straw in her only grandson's apple juice while he sang the vowel song in the background over the water he was running in the bathtub.

"You taught me to follow my instincts." I nodded, standing up straight and looking down at my phone.

"Not if your instincts are telling you to take a lady to a smoke-filled room." She was serious but I couldn't help grinning.

"The Sugar Shack is smoke-free, now," I said. "You should stop by and see it. Pops got a lotta upgrades."

"The day I step foot in that heathen haven is the day the Lord calls me home." She shot her eyes at me across the bar. "Now get on outta here before I yank that chain from around your neck. And don't bother coming to wake my baby up when you're done dancing or whatever you have up your sleeve. You can pick him up tomorrow."

"Yes, ma'am. I love you." I chuckled. My mama was a trip. "Love you, D!" I shouted down the hallway.

"Love you too, Daddy!" He yelled back as Mama blew me a kiss before I headed out the door.

She walked out of the door with a phone up to her ear, wearing a golden yellow knit dress that conformed to her curves and fell just below her knees, under a long-sleeved light blue denim jacket. High heels in the same color were strapped around her ankles adding at least four inches to her already long legs. I cleared my throat and my mind before stepping out of the car as she approached me, ending the phone call with a frown on her face.

"You good?" I asked, hoping the answer was yes.

"I will be." She rolled her eyes up to the sky, hurrying around to the passenger side where I met her to open the door.

She climbed in and eased into the seat on a sigh, seemingly more distracted than I'd bargained for. I pushed her door closed and said *"Shit."* On my way to the driver's side, shaking off my annoyance before reentering the car.

"Something you wanna talk about?" I wasn't gonna be able to move past it until I knew what I was moving past.

"Not really. It's just…baby daddy stuff." She blew out a breath, killing the screen on her cell and dropping it into a green clutch.

"I'm sorry. You must think I'm the rudest woman in the world. You look nice." She rolled her eyes to the side after letting her head fall against the headrest.

"Thanks." I nodded. "You look amazing."

"Stop."

"Come on. You know you do. That is unless you don't have mirrors in your house." I cranked the engine, taking a second to drink her in which brought a smile to her face.

"Flattery will get you nowhere, young man." That smile lingered and even influenced mine.

"It got you in the passenger seat of my ride." I winked, backing out of the driveway and heading to the Sugar Shack.

It was no surprise that we landed in the parking lot of a club that was as old as the land it was built on. The Sugar Shack was notorious for hosting fish fries for folks who couldn't afford funeral expenses and parties for folks who couldn't afford to celebrate anywhere else. I'd only been inside the place once or twice in my life. And both of those times I left with the scent of cigarette smoke in my hair. The last time stood out the most in my mind because I left the parking lot under a hail of bullets and I promised God that if he got me home alive that night, I would never step foot in the Sugar Shack again.

And now I was a liar.

Because with the way Damien looked rounding the front of his car in those dark denim jeans and that cream-colored sweater with the gold chain hanging off his neck, my smitten ass was willing to follow him anywhere, even through a ring of fire, if I'm being completely honest.

It was sad.

So so sad.

"What's wrong? You scared?" He had the nerve to crack that half-assed smile as he reached down to help me climb out of his car.

"I am God's child. Scared is not in my vocabulary." I took his hand, accepting the soft firmness of his grip as an invitation to feel even safer.

Once I'd planted my feet on the pavement, he pulled my arm up over my head and spun me around, an action I probably would've objected to had he asked if it was okay first. We walked up to the door with my hand in his, the breeze blowing over my bare shoulders cooling all of the spots that he had warmed. The sound of our footsteps crashing against the gravel became a soundtrack that I'd likely play over and over again long after this night was through.

We could hear the music before the door even opened. Johnny Taylor was down to his last two dollars, swearing that he wasn't gonna lose 'em. There was no one at the bar and the dance floor was empty. But I didn't mind. Crowded spaces weren't really my cup of tea.

"Briscoe, how botcha?" An older man behind the ticket booth looked up from his phone and smiled, displaying a big gold tooth that stuck out farther than the others.

"Wassup, Uncle Charles. Pop still lettin' you run that register?" Damien stepped away from me to be pulled into a dap and hug from the older gentleman who'd come from behind the cashier stand.

"He ain't got but two hands. He gotta let me do somethin'!" Uncle Charles laughed from his gut, eyes squinting, gold tooth blinging super hard. "What you got here, neph?" Now Uncle Charles's squinty eyes were on me.

"My bad. This is Angela. Angela, this is Uncle Charles." Damien returned to my side, smiling harder than I'd ever seen him smile since I met him.

"That's a beautiful name." Uncle Charles hiked a bushy brow. "To go with a beautiful lady." He reached for my hand, pulling it up to that gold tooth and planting a kiss on it. And all I could do was try to think of a way to sneak off and drench my hands in hand sanitizer.

"Nice to meet you, Uncle Charles," I said without thinking.

"Well look at that. She done already made herself family!" Uncle Charles laughed out loud again. "This one might be a keeper, Neph. Lemme get y'all a seat."

"We got it, Unc." Damien clapped his uncle's shoulder, taking my hand back into his and leading us past a velvet red rope.

"That wasn't too much, was it?" He leaned to the side and whispered in my ear, sending a chill down my spine that didn't stop until it hit the tips of my toes.

"No." I raised my shoulders in response, trying and failing to rid myself of these inappropriate tingles. "He's funny."

"And a flirt." I looked up to see Damien's brows hike.

"Look at you. Scared Uncle Charles is gonna steal your lady!"

Lord, what did I just say?

"Oh. So, you're my lady now?"

Dammit, he noticed!

"For the next few hours, I guess." I'd already stepped into it. Might as well put the whole thing on.

Damien shook his head and left it alone and I was so glad that he did.

"There's somebody else I want you to meet before we head to our seats." He tugged my hand and walked toward the bar where a handsome, much older man with the same dark eyes and full lips as Damien was standing with a phone perched between his ear and shoulder, fussing at somebody about something.

"You know what, how about I just call you back when you actually have the money? 'Cause right now you sound like somebody working for the march of dimes and I'm not runnin' no charity organization over here." He tipped his head up when he noticed me and Damien nearing him, then he said a few cuss words and hung up the phone.

"These motha fuckas." He blew out a breath, wiping his forehead with a white washcloth. "I'm sorry, son. How y'all doin'?" He came from the back of the bar, heading down a set of three steps and landing in front of us.

"Wassup, Pops?" Damien smiled, again, pulling his father into the same hug he'd just pulled his uncle into.

When they parted, Damien stepped up beside me and said, "This is the lady friend I was telling you about, Angela. Angela, this is my father, James Briscoe."

"Nice to meet you." I extended for a handshake, not surprised at all when Mr. Briscoe pulled my hand to his lips just like his brother.

"Pleasure's all mine, sweetheart." His subtle smile was identical to his son's, seasoned with deep creases at the corners of his moon-shaped eyes.

"What're y'all drinking tonight?" He asked, releasing my hand and shuffling back behind the bar, flipping that white towel over his shoulder like he'd done it a million times.

"Crown and Coke," Damien answered on a single breath as we approached the bar front.

"I'll just have some cranberry juice." I curled my lips to the side. "I don't drink."

"Well, that's a good sign." Mr. Briscoe winked at his son who didn't seem surprised or off-put by what I'd just disclosed.

He poured our drinks with smooth precision, knowing exactly when to pull back on the Crown in one hand while pressing the Coke tab on drink dispenser with the other. A handful of crystal-clear ice cubes clanked against the round, heavy-bottomed class before he filled it up with cranberry juice, dropping a cherry and a straw right in the center before he slid the drinks in front of us, still wearing that cocked smile.

"I don't know if y'all were planning on eating here tonight, but Tillie's got fried chicken wings on the menu." He nodded, eyes sweeping between the two of us as if he was sizing up our compatibility. And a part of me, I mean a deep-down part that I never showed to anybody, hoped that he saw something.

"I wasn't planning on getting my fingers greasy, but I'd be a fool to pass on Tillie's wings," Damien said, and all of a sudden my stomach was growling.

"Just let me know when you're ready and I'll put that order in." Mr. Briscoe nodded. "I got y'all set up over in the corner." He pointed to a dark spot at the other end of a wide dance floor. "Figured you might want some privacy."

"'Preciate it, Pops." Damien tipped his chin. "You ready?" He squeezed my hand and looked down at me.

"Yeah," I said. "I'm gonna go to the ladies' room first though." He squeezed my hand again before I went on my way and I could feel his eyes on my behind like two heated beams.

A neon orange sign just beyond the bar lit the way to the restroom and what I'm assuming was the kitchen based on the undeniably delicious smell swimming down the short hallway. I flipped out my phone to make sure I hadn't missed any emergency calls from my baby since she was spending the weekend with her father and the woman that he'd moved in with after only knowing her for two months. It didn't bother me so much that Paul had moved on. We'd been divorced for a year and moving on was expected for the both of us. But I was protective when it came to our baby girl. Fought him tooth and nail when he asked if it was okay for her to meet his little girlfriend. After a few rounds of begging and even granting my request to sit and talk with the woman first, I finally surrendered and let my baby go.

That still didn't stop me from stalking her every move. I'd taught her how to text me from her iPad and it's just my luck that my baby's a tiny genius. According to a message she'd sent all of five minutes ago, she and her daddy were eating pizza while her stepmother got caught up on Housewives of WhereverTheHell.

"Penny? Is that you?" A familiar voice sounded from over my shoulder and the last thing I wanted to do was turn around and confirm it.

But I had no choice. The hall was too narrow to look anywhere else.

"Sister Bimage?" I turned around and put a hand to my chest. And I don't know who was more shocked to see whom.

"I knew that was you!" She smiled that big, bright smile that made her buttery cheeks turn red.

"What are you doing here?" We both asked at the same time, then laughed.

"I was, um. I'm here with a friend." I cleared my throat, glancing over her shoulder to make sure Damien hadn't come looking for me.

"Oh, ok." She nodded; light eyes flooded with judgment.

"And you?" I straightened my posture after noticing that I'd slumped my shoulders in shame when I absolutely had no reason to.

Hell, I'm grown.

"Oh, I was, um… My sister, Tillie, works here." She explained. "She makes the best collards and fried chicken and I had to stop by and pick up my order before the riff-raff showed up."

"Oh, okay." I nodded, making a mental note to group text Chad and Jada as soon as I got in the restroom.

"Well, I don't wanna hold you up." She hurried. "I'll see you Sunday."

"Not if I see you first!" I joked and she laughed, moving with the speed of a turtle on skates trying to get out of my sight.

I rushed into the restroom and pulled my phone from my clutch.

Me: Y'all, please be up!

Less than five seconds passed before I got a response.

Jada: Up for what? Bible study?

Me: Better. I just ran into Sister Bimage and she is NOT cooking those collards that Daddy loves so much!

It was childish and petty to be ratting out my Daddy's secret girlfriend. But I didn't care. This was as close to some juicy gossip as I'd gotten in a long time.

Jada: So, where's she gettin' 'em from? And how would you know? You barely go anywhere.

Me: Her sister makes 'em. Apparently, she's the soul food plug out here.

Chad: How do you even know what a plug is?

Me: I am not that damn old!

Jada: But you IS!

Chad: Wait, which sister are you talking about, Penny? She got like three.

Me: Tillie.

Jada: You mean Miss Tillie from the Sugar Shack? Bitch, are you at the Sugar Shack????

Damn. I was so anxious to snitch on Sister Bimage that I didn't factor in the fact that I'd be snitching on myself too.

Chad: Penny, you at the Sugar Shack, sis? My nigga done finally walked down the Heathen's Hallway!

Jada: The Heathen's Hallway? Now that's some funny shit! LMMFAO.

Chad: You like that?

Jada: LOVE!

Chad: (CRYING)

Jada: Penny, where you at?

Chad: Probably drinkin' Crown Apple with a nigga named Pokey.

Jada: NIGGA!!!!

Me: I hate y'all. Bye!

Jada: They call me Pokey!

Chad: Big Pokey Beeeear! Awe yeah!

I shook my head laughing, knowing that it was gonna be ten times worse once they saw me in person. I was really slacking on my snitching skills. These two were not gonna let me make it.

"Aye, you good? Thought you went back there and climbed out the window."

"And miss out on Tillie's chicken wings? I think not!" She slid into the booth beside me, all winded like she'd just run from the bathroom.

"Really?" I slanted my eyes down at her, kinky hair extensions adding a little spice to her already sexy look. "You okay with getting your hands greasy? Not afraid of what I might think?"

"Sweetheart, believe me, the last thing on my mind when I'm wrist-deep in fried chicken wings is your judgment or anybody else's." She chuckled and took a sip from her cranberry juice.

"Especially now that I have proof that they're good." She put her glass down on the table.

"What proof? You smuggled a sample from the kitchen?" I hiked a brow, taking a sip from my Crown and Coke.

"Even better." Her eyes widened like she'd just cracked an age-old code. "Remember when I told you about Sister Bimage?"

"Yeah. The one who was trapping your pops with collard greens?" I squinted.

"Yes." She pressed her hands together, elbows resting on top of the table as she popped her lips and continued. "Well, guess who ain't cooked not a one pot of collards and is passing her sister's cuisine off as her own?"

I shook my head and waited for her to answer.

"Sister Bimage, that's who." She smirked. "This woman has been filling my father's belly in Jesus's name with food that hasn't touched her pots."

"Wow!" I tried matching her excitement before taking another sip from my drink.

"My sentiments exactly." She shook her head, leaning against the booth's backing.

"So, you gonna rat her out?" I asked, leaning back next to her, the soft scent of vanilla dancing off her brown skin.

"Nah." She shrugged a shoulder. "If I tell on her I gotta tell on myself and I already made that mistake texting my sister and brother."

"So, that's what you were in there doing? Snitching?" I turned my head sideways to look her in the face.

"What? I had to tell *somebody*." Her voice hiked.

"But you didn't." I chuckled. "Church folk. Y'all are somethin' else."

"I have no defense." She raised a pointer finger, swiping it down my nose, having no idea what the slightest touch from her did to me.

Caught in the suspension of her smile and her stare, we sat there for a moment, frozen in time, looking into each other's eyes with nothing there but the music to remind us that we weren't in outer space. I grabbed her finger and kissed it, watching her shiver in response and naming it my greatest accomplishment. Angela's walls were falling down, and she didn't even know it. She was shedding that tough exterior right before my eyes.

"You have beautiful teeth. You know that?" She said out of nowhere.

"What?" I smiled hard as hell, a thing I rarely ever did.

"Your teeth, they're like pearls. You don't show them nearly enough. Why is that?" Her stare was too intense. Had me straightening in my seat, hyper-aware of my posture and all kinds of other shit.

"I'on't know." I shrugged. "Not too big on smiling, I guess."

"But you're smiling right now." She noted.

"Because you make me want to." I disclosed without thinking, mentally slapping myself upside the head the minute the words left my mouth.

"Ten-piece spicy?" Miss Tillie showed up at the table in the nick of time, carrying a hot plate of fries and wings.

"That's us," I said, excitedly, pulling my eyes away from Angela who was still smiling and likely not done with our conversation.

"Smells delicious." Angela bit down on her bottom lip, eyes down on the plate of wings that Miss Tillie placed on the table in front of us.

"Thank you, baby." Miss Tillie nodded. "I thought my sister was pulling my leg when she told me Preacher and Laurie's daughter was out here. And with my Damien of all people." Miss Tillie patted me on the shoulder before kissing me on the cheek. She'd been working at the Sugar Shack since I was old enough to remember and was more like family than anything else.

"I'm sorry, you know my parents?" Angela straightened her back and leaned forward, squinting at Miss Tillie.

"Oh, yes." Miss Tillie propped a hand on her hip. "Me and your people go way back, baby. Your mama and daddy used to be regulars in here before he got that church up and running. Laurie used to sing right up on that stage every Saturday night. Girl used to have all these seats full."

I could see the wheels turning in Angela's head, and sat back before she went into the next question.

"Are you sure we're talking about the same people?" Angela asked. "My mother never told me anything about singing in the Sugar Shack."

"Ain't but one Laurie Barclay-Fold that I know of and she is definitely your mother. You got her eyes and I bet you got her hips hiding under that table." Miss Tillie laughed, and Angela couldn't help but smile.

"Wow!" Was the next word to leave Angela's lips. "I just...wow."

"Yeah." Miss Tillie nodded. "Well, if y'all need anything else, just let me know."

Miss Tillie started to turn away but Angela stopped her and said, "Actually, there is one thing. You wouldn't happen to have a picture of my mama? You know, onstage?"

"Oh, we got a dozen." Miss Tillie smiled wide. "Gimme a minute. Gotta go make sure my help ain't burning the pork chops. I'll be right back." She held up a finger and hurried away in a pair of white crocks that matched her white apron, pants and Sugar Shack T-shirt.

"You good?" Damien was so attentive, checking on me for the third time since we'd made it to the bottom of the most delicious plate of chicken wings I'd ever tasted.

"I told you, I'm fine." I offered a smile just to get one back. "The Sugar Shack has been full of surprises tonight. And I just…I guess I'm just tryna unpack it all."

"Can I make a suggestion?" He asked and I nodded yes, eyes widening as he slid out of the booth and stood beside the table with his hand extended.

"What?" I squeaked, thinking he must've lost his mind if he thought I was about to go anywhere near the dance floor with all the people that had trickled into this club.

"Come on. I know you ain't scared." He flashed that smile and I melted right down the center like a stick of butter under a hot knife.

India Arie's "Steady Love" was playing, which seemed safe enough for a woman who hadn't danced on an actual dance floor with an actual man since her wedding day. So I obliged, shedding my jacket and allowing Damien's big strong hand to pull me out of my seat and lead me to a dance floor sprinkled with enthusiastic steppers who were making moves that probably took years of chemistry to perfect. I couldn't have known what I was getting myself into based on the typically calm demeanor of my dance partner. But as soon as our feet hit the floor, he pulled me tight against his firm body, letting one hand fall to the rise of my hip, while the other tipped my chin so that all I could see was him.

Once I'd given him the attention he needed, he lowered his hand from my chin and rested it on my other hip. Side to side his palms guided me, pressed so tight against me I couldn't differentiate his heartbeat from my own. His steps were sure and fluid, in keeping with the rhythm like poetry in motion. I could not stop smiling and neither could he, staring down into my eyes as I draped my arms over his shoulders. Standing under the magic and the power that was Damien, I fell into his steps without even having to think. Our lips were so close that I could almost taste the Crown on his tongue. All I could think about was how good he must taste, but I didn't dare lean an inch farther. He tapped my waist and instinctively I knew that this signaled the arrival of an impending release. He pushed me away, holding the tips of my fingers, then spun me back into him, pulling a girlish giggle from my lips.

"That was cute." I smiled, pulling a foot up behind me. My body was on fire and his hands were to blame.

He didn't say a word, just kept staring at me like only he could. Was this what it felt like to be totally free? And would I only ever feel this way in his arms?

The song was nearing its end way too soon and I had no desire to abandon all that I was feeling to return to a booth where our bodies didn't touch. Verbalization of my thoughts didn't seem necessary at all as the instrumental to Robin Thicke's "I Need Love" began to play and Damien pulled me closer, as if closer was even possible.

And oh my God, he felt so good. Way too good for my own safety. And I'd promised myself that I wouldn't let this happen, but it seemed to be out of my hands. With his warm palms fitting perfectly where they lay and his warm breath against the tip of my nose as he stared into my eyes. It was completely embarrassing for my nipples to be as hard as they were. But there was nothing I could do to untie my body from his control.

Love was a word repeated at least fifty times for the duration of this song and it was a direct contradiction to what I was feeling inside. Lust would be more appropriate. Pure, steamy, unadulterated lust. Everything that I'd claimed not to be was raining down over my head and the head of the man who held me close right there in the middle of a dance floor for everyone to see.

And I didn't care.

Didn't for one second consider stopping his hands from traveling dangerously close to my behind before he stopped at the small of my back, showing way more restraint than me. Damien was showing me things on that floor. Proving that if he was capable of handling my body with this much precision while standing, there was no telling what he could do to me lying down. I'd fallen so deep into the *'broom closet'* that there wasn't a rope long enough to pull me out. And I couldn't blame anyone but my own damn self.

"Angela." He sighed against my lips as the song ended. I opened my eyes to find that we were the only two left on the floor and everyone else was sitting down watching.

"Huh?" I only had one breath left, and it floated right against his lips, just a whisper short of a kiss.

"It's getting late. I should get you home." He pressed his forehead to mine, speaking as if those weren't the words he actually wanted to say.

"Ok," I said, knowing that those weren't the words I'd wanted to hear either.

We both took a deep breath, blowing it out as we hesitantly parted from each other to hold hands and leave the dance floor with every eye on us.

Eight

The drive to her place from the Sugar Shack was quiet and loud all at the same time. I turned on the music to drown out my own thoughts but Jodeci was only making things worse. I had told myself this would happen if I didn't let up. That we'd wind up in this position, feeling things that we shouldn't, looking at each other as more than acquaintances who met for coffee every morning with nothing in common but a son and daughter who attended the same school.

But I didn't listen.

I ignored my better judgment and followed my instincts instead; listened to the loud voice inside my head that kept telling me to take a chance and stop fearing the fall. And look where it landed me. Driving down a long road, letting my playlist speak for me, hoping that she'd be brave enough to climb out of the car when I pulled up to her driveway because God knows that if she didn't, there'd be no more restraint left.

"Did you wanna stop for something to eat?" I asked though we'd had our fill of chicken.

80

"No, thank you." She said, glancing at me before turning her head to look out the window as we approached her street. "Those wings should keep me full until this time tomorrow night."

The street light bounced off her cheek as she smiled, eyes low and sleepy, visibly worn out.

"I had a nice time tonight, Damien." She sighed as we pulled into her driveway.

"Good. I did too." I said, rolling my head to the side to get a good look at her before we parted ways. "Lemme walk you to your door." I unbuckled my seatbelt, or at least I started to before her hand landed on my thigh.

"Actually, I don't wanna go in there." She said, lifting her hand from mine and rubbing it across her forehead.

"Then where do you wanna go?" I asked a question that I knew the answer to. An answer that I couldn't refuse because I damn sure wanted the same thing.

She didn't reply verbally, but the look in her eyes said it all. No smiling, no laughing, just a gaze that cut through my bones. And without further prompting necessary, I backed out of her driveway and headed to my place.

I'd put Shawndelle out after the first week when she came in drunk and passed out in DJ's bed. It was a stupid idea to have her staying with us anyway. The chick was toxic in every way and my son didn't need to be exposed to it. He had questions, of course, and I answered as honestly as I could. But no matter how soft or hard the truth was delivered, he was a child and at the end of the day, all he wanted was to know his mama loved him.

In any event, I wouldn't be entertaining that conversation with Angela. I was lucky that I wouldn't have to explain a grown woman camped out on my couch. She stood in the living room, canvasing everything, probably tryna figure out who I had coming over to clean up when the answer to that was me.

"You want something to drink? Water? Apple juice? A green smoothie?" I asked, pulling her eyes away from the drawing DJ had left on the coffee table for me before I dropped him off at Mama's.

"No. I'm good." She replied, the expression on her face caught somewhere between nervous and anxious. "Did your baby draw this?" She looked down at the picture that was folded in half with a green tree on one side and an orange one on the other.

"Yeah. He leaves me gifts in exchange for the stuff I'm always bringing home from the ABE Market." I replied, walking over to where she was standing in front of my sofa.

"How sweet." She smiled. "That's pretty detailed for a five-year-old. Did you ask him what it meant?" She slid her eyes up to me, thick kinky locs laying on her bare shoulders, gold charm resting at the center of her chest.

"Always." I nodded, leaning over to pick up the picture. "The green one symbolizes the good days and the orange one symbolizes the bad."

"Wow, that's…deep." She hiked a brow. "How does he know the difference?"

I shrugged my shoulders and put the picture back on the table then looked into her eyes and said, "I didn't ask."

She bit down on her bottom lip, leaving that subject where it was to hopefully lean toward the one that had brought her to my place.

"So, what do you usually do on a Friday night?" I flopped down on the sofa and flipped on the TV. I didn't want her to think that I expected anything no matter how hard it was to look at her without having a physical reaction.

"Not this." She sat down next to me, letting her head fall back against the cushions.

"And what is *this*?" I rested my head so that it was close to hers then rolled it to the side to look at her.

"You know what this is, Damien. Don't act like you don't do this all the time."

"Wow! That's the most presumptuous shit I've ever heard you say." I chuckled.

"What? I didn't mean to—"

"It's cool." I sat forward, resting my elbows on my thighs. "And for the record, I don't do this all the time." I looked back to find her eyes on me.

"I'm sorry." She sighed, leaning forward and resting her chin on my shoulder. "Will you forgive me?" She pouted. And I'd forgive a thousand sins if she kept on looking at me like that.

"What am I forgiving you for?" I asked because giving in would be too simple.

"For assuming that you be havin' hoes." She cracked a smile and all I could do was laugh. Couldn't believe those words had left her mouth.

"You're crazy, you know that?" I planted a kiss on her forehead, having no idea what led me to do so. Her natural reaction was to nestle her chin deeper into my shoulder which left me no choice but to crane my neck and gauge her expression before turning sideways and planting my hand on both sides of her face.

"Angela?"

"Yeah?"

"I wanna kiss you."

"Then do it."

Her lips parted and her eyes remained locked on mine, chest rising and falling, nipples beading beneath her dress. I scrunched my hands in her hair, and pulled her lips to mine, parting them with my tongue, finally getting a chance to taste her.

And she was perfect.

So much better than the sweetness I'd been imagining and playing on a loop in my mind since the first time she sat across the table from me. Gravity was escaping me and I was sinking through the floor, swallowing her up as she reciprocated the untamed lashing of my tongue.

Hungrily, I slid my hands down the base of her neck, applying just enough pressure to express possessiveness. I needed her to understand that even if it was for one night if she surrendered to me just once and never wanted to speak to me again, she was mine to please and I took that shit seriously.

Words escaped us as our tongues remained tangled, panting down each other's throats, hearts racing, bodies curling into an inferno with no desire to be extinguished. The warmth and precision of her little hands sliding under my sweater forced me to move with more urgency and an abandon of restraint. I pulled my hands away from her neck to roll my sweater up and off, falling back against the sofa when she pushed me and jumped on my lap. Blood rushed to my head and my dick jumped under my jeans in response to the softness of her ass pressing against my thighs.

"You are so beautiful." She moaned. And I had never been called beautiful by anyone in my life.

It felt strange but sexy all at the same time. Had me grinning like a mother fucker and ready to rip that dress off her ass.

So, I did.

Rolled it right up her thighs, exposing the prettiest chocolate skin that I'd ever wanted to taste. She slid it up the rest of the way, uncovering her flat tummy and beautiful breasts, nipples sitting erect, begging me to take them into my mouth.

And I did that shit too.

Because who was I to deny any part of her body of being sucked, kissed, and pleased?

"Damien!" She cried out my name, grinding against my shit, back caving as I alternately sucked her nipples until they became engorged inside my mouth.

I roped my arms around her waist, squeezing her ass and pulling her harder against me until I could no longer resist standing up and wrapping her legs around my waist.

I rushed us to the bedroom, kicking out of my shoes in record speed before laying her down on the bed and taking her in wearing nothing but a pair of bikini-cut panties and the glow of a woman in need. My staring made her nervous and she couldn't deny it if she wanted to with that smile on her face.

She asked, "What are you staring at?"

And I replied, "You." before reaching into a drawer in my nightstand and retrieving a condom.

Saying you're ready and *being* ready are two completely different things. And I learned that lesson the hard way when Damien dropped his boxer briefs. A thick muscle dipped in chocolate with veins traveling from base to tip had my mouth watering, flesh growing weak, and all the praying in the world wouldn't help me close my eyes. I lie there in his bed with cool sheets against my back, still wearing the golden chain with the feather charm around my neck that was supposed to keep me out of this situation in the first place. Instead, it had charmed a man, and quite honestly charmed me. Yeah, I had to blame my jewelry because there was no way I'd be held accountable for what was about to take place.

Like a lion stalking his prey, Damien approached me at the foot of the bed. His hardened flesh swung between his toned legs, sheathed in latex and nothing else. Dark brown nipples hardened at the center of his pecs. And it was all I could do not to sit up and pull him on top of me. The smile that curved my lips in response to his heated gaze transformed into something more serious. More suitable for a grown-ass woman. With his eyes on me, penetrated the very center of my soul, I arched my back from the mattress offering a nonverbal request for him to hurry up and stop playing with my emotions. He snaked up the length of my slowly warming flesh, planting kisses on the insides of my ankles, up the insides of my thighs, lingering at the opening of my pussy lips before sucking my clit like a vacuum. I tried keeping quiet to somehow mask the fact that I hadn't been touched, let alone sucked there, in longer than I could remember. But my lips deceived me by flying open and shouting out his name like a sex-crazed lunatic who didn't know that worshipping an idol God was a sin.

"Damien!" I trembled against his wet lips, locking a hand behind his head and forcing his mouth harder against me as I rolled my hips up and down then back up again.

He felt so good that I couldn't let go. I knew the man needed to breathe but my legs clamped closed. I grinded against his face until the bubble swelling in my belly popped, sending me into a fit of shivers that were beyond my control.

And he didn't say a word, smiling that half-smile when he looked up at me coming out of the other end of an orgasm that would've been jotted down in my journal of unregretted sins if I had one. He kissed the tenderness that was my sex as if to say goodbye. But then he didn't leave, sliding his long, thick body up on top of mine, and slipping in between my folds with a thrust that set everything inside me ablaze.

"Fuck!" I screamed. *Screamed* at the top of my lungs. Vulgarity was the only means to express how open I was at that moment. There was no room for pretty words or good manners.

Wide and hard, he swelled against my walls, pulling tears from my eyes that I'd have to explain later. Composure was a thing that I'd left outside his door. And this was a version of myself that had been under lock and key.

"Damien!" I cried real liquid tears, begging for mercy that I didn't really want. "Please!" I whimpered, pain and pleasure tugging me in either direction as he stroked me deep, and long, and hard, sucking my earlobe into his wet mouth.

"You feel so good." He whispered, rumbling baritone vibrating against my neck, I tightened my legs around his waist to hold him as close as I possibly could.

"Shit, Angela!" He groaned, matching the rolling of my hips with rhythmic strokes that I'd already imagined when I saw the way he moved on the dance floor.

A heaviness weighed in my belly, and every stroke brought it closer to the surface. My eyes fell closed and he tugged at my hair, commanding me to keep them open.

"Look at me." He said, beautiful brown lips parting as he raised from my neck to stare down into my eyes. "I wanna see that pretty face when you cum." He said and that alone made my pussy pulsate.

"Aahhh." I couldn't even formulate words with him looking at me like that, so deep inside me that there wasn't room for anything else. "I can... I can't!" I didn't even know what the hell I was saying.

"Yes, you can." He shoved into me harder as if he somehow knew what I didn't.

"Let go." He laid into me, forcing my legs up and open wider. "I got you." He said with a sureness that gave me no choice but to believe.

I let my thighs fall apart, and my good sense too, digging my nails into his back as he pumped between my legs. My mouth was dry from being so wide open, eyes locked into a stare that felt safer than it should. Damien was taking me completely. Driving me all the way over the age. My head smashed against the headboard and then a scream shot from my lips.

"Oh my God!" I didn't mean to say it. I knew better than to use the Lord's name in vain. But I couldn't help it. I wasn't even in the room at this point. I had floated somewhere else beyond the clouds and all the rules.

"Angela, baby!" He kept on stroking, still staring at me with beads of sweat forming on his forehead. "Aahhh!" He ground into me, reaching my spot and banging it loose.

"I can't!" My nails sank into his skin, tears cascading down the sides of my face as the pressure building inside me quickly came to a head. "Please. Oh, please!" I cried out as he kept stroking until finally, I arrived and exploded where I lay.

Only then did his eyes fall closed as he sped up the stroke, banging me harder without letting up. Damien sucked his teeth, grinding his abs against my belly, succumbing to the tightening of my walls around his flesh and releasing his warm spend inside of me.

We lie there for a minute afterward, neither of us knowing what to say. She might not believe me if I said it, but this wasn't how I expected the night to end. I didn't regret it. At least not yet. Not with her warm body so close to mine and her wild hair on my chest reminding me that she was just as human as me and not some mortal created by the church.

Still, I knew that morning would come. And no matter how many rounds we had left in us, it was highly likely that once she walked out of the door, her conscience would get the better of her and she'd never speak to me again. I'm not gonna lie, the thought of that messed with me a little. But it was what it was. I'd been dealt worse hands. As for now, I had to enjoy her while I had her.

"Where are you goin'?" Her voice grumbled against my chest when I tried to slide her off of me so I could go empty my bladder.

"To piss," I replied. "Thought you were asleep."

"I was until you tried to take my pillow." She smiled up at me, blinking her eyes, big kinky locks falling into her face.

"I'll bring it back when I'm done." I pushed her hair away and planted a kiss on her lips, the sweet scent of her arousal still present after I'd left it on her tongue.

"Hurry up." She said, rolling onto my side of the bed when I got up, pretty brown titties on full display, nipples pebbling in response to the sixty-eight-degree temp in my bedroom.

I shook my head and footed to the restroom; dick heavy in my hands, though my balls were five pounds lighter. Angela had no idea how long it'd been since I'd had that kind of release. But from the tightness of her pussy, I could tell it had probably been longer for her.

"What color is this paint on your walls? It's so calming." She yelled from the bed while I stood at the sink, washing my hands and staring into the mirror at a man who couldn't believe there was a woman in his bed that he didn't wanna put out.

"Slate-gray," I replied, flipping off the light switch and heading back over to the bed. "Almost looks blue in the daytime," I added, dick slapping the inside of my thigh as I eased down next to her, laid on my back and pulled a hand behind my head.

"I'd like to see that." She said, resuming her position with her head on my chest.

"Is that your way of saying you wanna stay the night?" I tilted my eyes down, catching a nervous smile on her face.

"Yeah. But only if you want me to." She bit down on her bottom lip, smile doubling in size when I pulled her up on top of me.

"I'll take that as a yes!" She looked down into my eyes.

"Damn right." I reached around and smacked her ass, before retrieving a condom from my drawer, ripping it open and sliding it on.

Angela was already wet for me, raising her hips then sliding down over my shit, pulling a moan from my mouth that I couldn't swallow.

"Shit!" My head fell back against the pillow, hands gripping her sides as my knees fell apart. She rolled her hips back and forth, staring down into my eyes, giving me everything I needed with no instructions necessary.

And then she leaned back, palms braced on my thighs, throwing that pussy up and at me like she'd been built to do it. I couldn't even close my mouth, locked into a stare of surrender and defeat in my own damn bed. If this was a competition of who was getting fucked, my black ass was lying here losing.

"You like this pussy?" Wait, now she was talking? Who the fuck was this woman and where the hell was she hiding the church girl?

"Tell me." She pleaded; voice soft yet demanding. "Tell me you like it, Damien. Say it, baby, please!"

"I love it!" I overshot because I'd passed liking her pussy twenty strokes ago. "I love it, baby." I rose my hips from the bed, driving deep inside her warmth, wishing I could stay there forever.

Her knees dug into the mattress when she sat up and rode me, hips swirling like a serpent, pussy lips wide open taking every inch. She leaned forward, planting her palms on my chest, panting and moaning as I thrust into her deep. Her nipples were so close to my mouth that I couldn't help pulling them between my teeth, sucking them until they were solid against my tongue before licking them to soothe the sting.

"Oh!" She cried out, back arching as she kept on riding, a wild mass of coils falling over her face. She was beautiful in a way that I'd never be able to describe. Perfect and angelic, yet capable of snatching my soul.

Pulling my knees together, I laid back and let her ride me, watching those perky chocolate mounds bouncing before my eyes. And then it became too much of a challenge to keep my hands to myself, I gripped her ass and guided it up and down my shaft while she slammed her palms against the headboard.

"Get that shit!" I slid her up and down my dick, taking a nipple into my mouth as she rocked back and forth. "Ride it, baby," I mumbled against her chest, losing all composure when she sat back up.

"You're so deep." She trailed her tongue across her lips, eyes glossed with lust and the need to come undone. "I'm gonna cum all over you." She let her mouth fall open, slamming down onto me harder, breasts bouncing up and down.

"Give it to me," I begged, raising from the bed, back pressed against the headboard as she kept on riding me hard. "Gimme all that sweet pussy." I roped my arms around her waist, pulling her tight against me, feeling my dick tap the bottom.

"Fuck!" Her verbal reaction was validation that I had, in fact, tapped that spot.

"Damien, please!" She begged for something she couldn't name. Something we both needed desperately and would be getting in due time.

"Look at me." I leaned my head back as she ran her fingers through her hair.

"Angela?" Her eyes fell closed, and I wasn't having that shit.

"Open your eyes, baby," I commanded and she obliged, displaying those deep brown marbles that had me abandoning common sense.

"Yeah." I groaned, shoving in and out then back into her again. "Fuck yeah!" My knees shivered as her thighs did the same, imploding, exploding, and unraveling all over again.

Nine

He was right, the walls did look blue when the sun shone through the window. And the fact that I was witnessing this meant that we'd slept the night away. His sheets felt like heaven, soft and warm against my skin. I rolled over on my side to find that Damien wasn't there. There was no need to be alarmed though, with the scent of bacon and eggs seeping through the cracked bedroom door. An empty glass sitting on the nightstand reminded me of how parched we'd become after making love. I sat up and pulled the covers up to my chest, canvasing the room in search of my dress. When I didn't locate it, I climbed out of bed and footed to the restroom to see if it was in there.

If I had any questions about the glow that I was feeling, it was present on my face as I stood in front of the mirror. My hair was a mess scattered all over my head and my nipples were still tender from being licked, sucked and bitten. Still unable to find my dress, I grabbed a white T-shirt that had been neatly folded and left on the edge of the sink and slid it on. I figured it was for me. Damien just seemed like the type to hide a woman's clothes so he could see her frolicking around in his.

After using a finger and some toothpaste to give my teeth a hoe-brushing, I rinsed and spat then hiked a brow, wondering if I was hearing things coming from outside the bedroom door. A woman's voice going back and forth with Damien had me looking harder for my dress and even harder for my heels in case some shit was about to jump off. I found neither and decided to suck it up and head my ass out of the room.

"Is everything ok?" I emerged from the hallway to find a short, frail, light-skinned sister standing in front of Damien with silky brown hair hanging down to her behind.

"Yeah." Damien quickly replied. "This is my son's mother." He tilted his head back, staring up at the ceiling like she was the last person he wanted me to see.

"Oh, so, I don't have a name now?" The woman smirked at Damien before turning her eyes to me. "I'm Shawndelle. And you are?"

"None of your damn business," Damien answered before I could. "She was just leaving. I'm sorry." He said to me.

"To go where Briscoe?" Shawndelle folded her arms across her chest, darting her eyes at Damien, almost as if she was about to cry.

"You know what, I... I'm just gonna head out," I said, wanting no parts of whatever the hell these two had going on. "Can I have my dress? I didn't see it in the bedroom." I folded my arms, suddenly hyperaware of how exposed my body was.

"Yeah, it's in the closet. But could you just wait a minute?" Damien begged. This had to be awkward for him. But it was more awkward for me.

I sighed, heading into the bedroom before him, stopping beside the bed as he walked in. "I know this looks crazy," He started as he walked to the closet to retrieve my dress. "And that's 'cause it is." He came out with my dress in hand. "But I wish you'd stay and put something in your stomach. We had a long night."

"Thanks. But I think you have bigger fish to fry right now." I slipped his T-shirt off, watching his eyes travel to my breasts before I dropped the dress on over my head.

"Last night was nice. I had a great time. Now I gotta go home." I said all of that on one breath, picking my heels up off the floor and leaving the room barefoot because the last thing on my mind was putting on some damn shoes.

"It was nice meeting you, Angela." Shawndelle felt the need to speak as I rushed past her in route to the door.

"Yeah. I'm sure it was." I looked her up and down, rolling my eyes from her to Damien before grabbing my clutch off the entry table and heading out of the door.

"Sorry."

"That you are."

"Look, I wouldn't've come back over here if I had anywhere else to go." Shawndelle stood in the living room with her arms crossed while I scraped breakfast onto the plates that were supposed to be mine and Angela's.

"You gonna eat all that?" She had the nerve to ask like it wasn't her fault that my damn company had left.

"What do you want from me, Shawndelle? And I don't mean shelter or food. I mean what do you really want? Why do you keep showing up at my door when you know I don't want you here? Cause it's getting old."

"I wanna be around my son."

"You wanna fuck with his head." I'd raised my voice, placing the plates on the dining table and taking a seat in the chair at the head of the table. "And I can't let you do that. Because unlike you, I actually love the kid."

"I love him too!" Now she'd raised her voice and joined me in the dining room, taking a seat in the chair to my left. "And I know I fucked up. I know I'm *always* fucking up. But it's different this time."

"What's different?" My fork clinked against the plate as I dug in to scoop up some eggs. "I found you drunk in his bed. He was cradling your head like you were the damn kid and he was the adult. Please tell me what makes that better than you not being here?"

"I wasn't drunk. I told you that." She defended, looking down at the food but not touching it.

"Then what do you call it? Was that not your puke in his trash can?"

"It was."

"And why were you throwing up if you weren't drunk?"

"Because I'm sick." She sighed, eyes roving up to the ceiling before lowering to look at me. "I have stage four cervical cancer with maybe three months to live."

I couldn't finish chewing the food in my mouth. Just swallowed it whole before I could open my mouth and say, "Are you serious?"

"Yeah." She nodded, clearing her throat. "That's why I came back home. That's why he sent me back home. 'Cause no nigga worth his weight in gold wants to be with a dying bitch."

"Shawn—"

"I don't need your pity, Briscoe." She raised a hand, voice shaky with emotion which wasn't typical for Shawndelle. "I just wanna...I just need to be around DJ before I leave here. And I know this is asking a lot, that's why I didn't wanna tell you in the first place. But honestly, it probably wouldn't've happened any other way. I've been trash at this whole mama thing and now all I wanna do is make it right."

I wasn't sure what I was supposed to say to that. I mean obviously, I couldn't kick her out. But what the hell was supposed to be next?

"I'm sorry. This is…it's fucked up."

"I know. But it is what it is. I've had longer to think about it than anybody else. Trust me, the shit hurts."

"Are you sure it's terminal? I mean they've come a long way with cancer research." I was digging deep to find some compassion. Nobody'd ever hurt me as bad as Shawndelle, but she didn't deserve to die. Not at thirty-five years old.

"I've been battling this for a whole year, Briscoe." The sadness in my eyes was hard as hell to look at. "At this point, I'm just tired. Tired of experimenting. Tired of getting my hopes up. It's all just prolonging the inevitable and it's physically and mentally draining."

"Man." My shoulders slumped; appetite gone down the damn drain.

"Yeah." She sighed, slouching back into the chair.

"We gotta tell him." I decided before thinking too long.

"What? He's five." Her eyes scrunched with concern, a thing I'd never seen her express for our son before today.

"Yeah. But he's smart." I returned. "And resilient. And I don't lie to him about anything because he deserves better than that."

"But I—"

"You can stay here." I cut her off. "And the only condition is that you agree to tell my son the truth and not string him along on some fairytale before you leave him again. It's the least you can do."

"You act like I'm leaving him on purpose. I'm dying, Briscoe. Literally."

"And I'm not happy about that. Trust me. I got plenty of reasons to hate you, but I would never wish death on nobody."

We sat there in silence, me looking down at the plate of food that I had no desire to eat, her picking at her nails, bouncing her knee under the table.

"You got proof of this before we go any further?" I had to ask because Shawndelle never had a problem with lying to my face.

"Yeah." She looked up at me. "I got a purse fulla meds. And if you need my PCP's number—"

"I do." I pushed back from the table and grabbed my plate. "You can leave it on the coffee table. The guest room's all yours." I headed into the kitchen to clean out my plate before going into my bedroom to somehow digest all of this and get ready for the day.

Me: Can you talk?

I thought about calling but didn't wanna be inconsiderate since I didn't know what she did with her days when she wasn't sitting in the coffee shop with me. She didn't reply although she'd read the text message, so I decided to leave it alone and let her come around on her own.

"Why you sitting over there lookin' like somebody scrubbed yo' balls with a brillo pad?" Uncle Charles came out of the supply closet at the Sugar Shack holding a box of new drinking glasses to slide on the shelf behind the bar.

"Wassup, Unc?" I looked up from my phone, laying it down on top of the bar next to my glass of ice water.

"Ain't shit." He huffed. "Your big-headed ass daddy got me in here working like a Hebrew slave."

"And paying you like one too if you break them damn glasses." Pops came through the flapping doors that led to the kitchen. We'd already chopped it up and I'd been sitting at the bar listening to Bobby Blue Bland and looking stupid for the past fifteen minutes. "What we lookin' like on that Crown Apple?" Pops asked Uncle Charles, clipboard in his hand and a white towel thrown over his shoulder.

"Sac's was supposed to bring in a case." Uncle Charles answered. "Said something about the delivery truck having engine problems. Might have to go pick the Crown up from the store."

"Then what you sittin' yo' ugly ass around here for?" Pops slanted his eyes to his younger brother who was the only family he had left aside from their baby sister, Pearl Anne, who lived in New Orleans and rarely visited.

"I got a right mind to drop these glasses and stick my foot up yo ass." Uncle Charles threatened. And all I could do was sit there and laugh because I knew for a fact neither one of them would hurt a hair on the other's head.

"You ain't got a right mind to do shit." Pops huffed, throwing a hand and walking to the other end of the bar. "You in your car, D?" He asked me without looking back.

"Yes, sir," I replied, knowing what was coming next.

"Run your uncle down to Sac's to pick up that Crown. He can't see worth a damn and I ain't givin' him my keys." He sighed, unlocking the register and pulling out a checkbook.

"This should cover it." He reached across the bar and handed me a check. "And if Paul asks why the numbers look funny, tell him I'm charging his ass a delivery fee."

I took the check and waited for Uncle Charles to finish putting out the glasses, then stopped when he pulled a jacket off the coat rack.

"I think your friend left this here last night." Handing me a denim jacket that made my knees weak because it smelled just like Angela.

"Thanks." I took the jacket from his hands and headed out to the car.

"I'm shole glad you came, nephew. That box looked heavy as hell."

Uncle Charles didn't even bother getting out to open the door when I came out of Stac's Liquor store carrying a heavy ass case of Crown Royal.

"You ain't worth a quarter, Unc." I climbed into the driver's seat after loading the case in the trunk.

"Now you startin' to sound like your old man." He chuckled, bald head falling back against the headrest as he popped a hand full of peanuts in his mouth.

"You mind if we make one more stop?" I asked as if we weren't in my car.

"It's yo boat. Sail it!" He opened his bottle of Coke and took a sip before closing it, sitting it back in the cup-holder and refastening his seatbelt.

"Boy, it smell like a good time in here!" Uncle Charles never changed his tone no matter where we were. Walking into *The Hem* did smell inviting as shit, though. I could see why folks were dropping so much money to get their backs and beards rubbed.

"They give *'happy endings'* in here, nephew?" Uncle Charles asked, voice loud and boisterous like we were back at the Sugar Shack.

"No, we don't!" A voice as loud as his sounded from behind the receptionist's desk. "Is there anything else we can help you with?"

"Hi, Miss Davie." I cut in before she cursed my crazy uncle out. "Is Angela in? She left her jacket at the…she left her jacket. And I was just… I happened to be on this side of town, so, I thought I'd bring it by."

"On this side of town? Now that's a black ass lie." Uncle Charles ratted me out. "I can't remember the last time I came this close to the white folk's neighborhood on purpose."

"I see." Miss Davie cut her eyes at Uncle Charles. "And Angela's in but she's doing inventory. I can take it to her if you want?" She extended a plump hand, but I couldn't release the jacket because it would defeat the purpose of me driving twenty minutes out of my way.

"Actually, I was—"

"Is everything okay out here?" She rounded the corner wearing jeans and a sweater, looking relaxed, beautiful, and not worried about me.

"Yeah. The flower man has your jacket." Ms. Davie looked back over her shoulder, cutting her eyes at Angela before smiling at me.

"Hey." I looked over Miss Davie's shoulder at Angela. "You left this." I held up her jacket, head leaning to the side not giving a damn how stupid I looked.

"How're you doing, Uncle Charles?" She rolled her eyes from me to my uncle.

"I've been better. But I've also been worse." Uncle Charles grinned like a Cheshire cat, returning his eyes to Miss Davie.

The smile Angela'd given to my uncle disappeared when she returned her eyes to me.

"Thank you." She stepped forward beside Miss Davie, extending her hand over he receptionist's desk.

"Can we talk?" It's all I wanted.

"Damien, I don't—"

"Just a minute of your time. It's all I'm asking." I stood there holding her jacket in the bend of my arm, catching her eyes halfway between us and holding them there until she finally gave in.

"Miss Davie, can you get Uncle Charles something to drink?" Angela's eyes swept away from me.

"Yeah. Some of that sparkling white folk's water would be nice." Unc flashed that gold tooth and Miss Davie just shook her head.

"Can we make this fast? I don't wanna leave those two alone for too long, in case this Briscoe voodoo runs in the family and my receptionist disappears into your uncle's bed then wakes up to be greeted by one of his baby mamas."

"Damn. Did you practice that in the mirror?" He stepped into my office and pulled the door closed behind him.

"I didn't. And why are you closing my door?" I leaned my behind against my desk, planting my palms on either side of me.

"For privacy, obviously." He dropped my jacket on the small table beside the door. "Did you get my text?"

"What if I did?"

"I *know* you did."

"Then why did you ask?"

"'Cause you didn't reply."

"Am I obligated to reply?"

"You know what, I didn't come here to go back and forth." He dropped his shoulders and started walking toward me. And try as I might, I couldn't stop the butterflies from fluttering in my belly.

"Then why did you come, Damien?" Even saying his name made me heat up like a furnace. "Because it's clear that I didn't want you to."

"Is it, though?" He squinted his eyes, now standing so close that I could smell his crisp cologne. "You could've easily sent me outta here. You didn't even have to step out of your office. But you did."

"It's called customer service." I lied. "It's how I keep the doors open in this place."

"And what about this?" He ran the tip of his finger from the peak of my shoulder down the side of my arm. "Does every customer give you goosebumps?"

The nerve of this man.

Barging into my place of business with a God damn coat. Walking into my office and touching me like I belonged to him when we both knew damn well I didn't.

Or did I?

Lord, I was questioning myself. Why in the hell was I questioning myself? Having his baby mama show up unannounced like she did was my ticket out of this mess, and here I was falling back into it again.

"Why are you here?" I stood from leaning against the desk, stepping to the side to put some space between us.

"To tell you that I'm sorry." Was his simple reply. "And that I wanna see you again."

"Listen, last night was fun. *All* of it." I sighed, shivers running down my spine as images of his bronzed naked body flashed before my eyes. "But it doesn't seem like a good time for you to be seeing anybody."

"So, this is about my timing?" He pressed a hand to his chest displaying the pulsating veins running under his brown skin.

"Yes, it is." I raised my voice. "Do you know how awkward it was walking out of that room and seeing her there? It's embarrassing. But I don't expect you to understand that because it's probably all in day's work."

"Wait, what? What the hell is that supposed to mean?" He squeaked, staring down at me.

"Let's not play this game." I put my hands up, rounding the desk to take a seat in my chair. "Your life's a mess and I don't have time for that. We had a good time. Let's just leave it at that."

"You know what, you're right." He nodded his head, running a hand down his bearded chin. "But before I go, you should know that not only were you the first woman I've had in my bed since I got sole custody of my son, you're the one who asked to be in it in the first place."

"Excuse me—"

"I'm not finished." He cut me off, and it was a damn shame how much that turned me on. "I wanted you there just as much as you wanted to be there. And I want you there again, as stupid as that sounds. You're judgmental as fuck and probably don't give a damn about what I'm about to say, but my son's mother has three months to live and showed up at my door this morning begging to spend those three months with our son."

"Well…oh." Was all I could say. If this was some ploy to get me to eat my words, then he should probably know that it worked.

"That's…wow. I'm sorry to hear that." I inhaled and blew out a breath, dropping the pin that I'd picked up out of nervousness because I needed to do something with my hands.

"Yeah." He breathed in, chest rising and falling beneath a crisp white T-shirt. Probably the same one he'd left for me to put on and eat breakfast in. I bet it still smelled like me.

"Enjoy the rest of your day." He turned to walk away. And my heart fell into my stomach pulling me up and out of my chair.

"Does she have what she needs?" My voice was oozing with desperation. I didn't want him to leave any more than he wanted to go.

"I don't know. We haven't gotten that far into it." He turned around to reply, deep brown eyes carrying more weight than they should.

"Well, I know people. If she needs assistance, I can reach out." I offered because it was the right thing to do. The *Christian* thing to do, no matter what me and Shawndelle's common denominator was.

"Thanks. I'll let her know." He said without looking at me, and gripping the doorknob forcing me to step from behind the desk.

I had to think fast before he left. I'd said so many things I didn't mean. The last thing that I wanted was to never see his face again.

"Do you have plans tomorrow?" The words raced off my lips so fast my thoughts had to catch up.

"If you don't, the service starts at ten." I kept on when he didn't reply or look back. "We have children's church if you wanna bring DJ. And you could bring Shawndelle too. I doubt things can get more awkward than they did this morning."

He still hadn't said a word, and I had no choice but to accept his silence as he twisted the nob and pulled the door open, then walked out and pulled it closed behind him.

Ten

We had a packed house as usual, which didn't help to ease the nervousness rolling in the pit of my stomach thanks to the hurried invitation I'd extended to Damien and his family. I didn't know if he would come, and almost hoped that he wouldn't. I'd stuck my foot in my mouth with the shoe still on and had no idea how to deal with it.

"You ok? You look like you stole money from the collection plate?" Jada slid onto the pew right beside me and Patience, planting a kiss on her niece's cheek. She wouldn't be needed in the choir stand since this Sunday the male choir would be featured.

"I'm fine," I replied, looking over my shoulder for the tenth time, running a hand over Patience ribbon curls trying to play off the fact that I was looking for my guests.

"Well, you don't look it." Jada looked up from her phone, dropping it in her lap as she smirked at me. "If you're hiding from somebody, I got you."

"I am not hiding. I just…oh Lord." I looked back at the chapel doors again. And this time, I saw what I was looking for.

"Oh, Lord what?" Jada followed my line of sight. "Wait, is that…is that Briscoe?" She squinted.

"I didn't know he was married." She poked her lips out and returned her eyes to me. "Guess you won't be tapping that after all." She shrugged her shoulders and went back to texting on her phone.

"Jada!" I covered Patience's ears and cut my eyes at my sister.

"My bad." She looked up at me from the corner of her eye, knowing she got on my damned nerves.

"Daddy, that's Patience's mama!" I heard DJ from the back of the church. "Can we go sit up there? Please, Daddy?" He begged, pulling Damien's hand.

Damien surrendered, unable to tell his son no. And within the next minute, the trio was standing beside our pew.

"Hey, Patience!" DJ screamed, pulling Patience's eyes up from the sketch app her uncle Chad had downloaded on her iPad.

"DJ! You got on a suit!" She dropped the iPad in my lap and jumped up to hug her friend. "How did you get to my Paw Paw's church?" She asked him as they stood there in the middle of the narrow walkway like there weren't two grown adults behind them waiting to take their seats.

"We took I-45 to the beltway. It was easy." DJ answered like a man ten times his age.

"Baby, why don't you and DJ have a seat so Mr. Damien and Miss Shawndelle can get by." I stood up to help the little people onto the pew. "Good morning." I greeted a calm looking Damien and a nervous-looking Shawndelle.

"Good morning." They both said, squeezing past Jada, then the kids, and then me.

"I'm sorry, Shawndelle this is my sister Jada. Jada this is Shawndelle. Damien's,"

"Baby mama." Shawndelle picked up the ball where I dropped it. "Nice to meet you." She looked past me to offer a kind smile to my sister.

"Oh, ok. Nice to meet you too." Jada smiled back, crossing her leg like she was relaxing into some gossip.

Just as we'd gotten settled, whispers started scattering all around the church. I had an idea who walked in but turned around to look anyway. And there came in my little brother walking in with his beautiful girlfriend, Miss Taya Maxey.

"Wassup, Jay?" He approached the pew and planted a kiss on Jada's cheek, and Patience, of course, came right back out of her seat.

"Uncie Chad!" She slid past Jada and opened her little arms. He leaned down and picked her up, holding her along the side of him.

"Bertha." He looked down at me and grinned.

"Chadwick." I shook my head as he slid in with his lady following close behind. "Hey, Taya." I extended my hand to meet hers since space was too limited for our routine hug.

"Is that... That's Taya Maxey! You didn't tell me we were gonna be sitting next to Taya Maxey!" Shawndelle punched the side of Damien's arm and struggled to keep her composure.

Jada laughed and I covered my smile as Taya graciously slid past us to go and give Shawndelle a calming hug.

"It's nice to meet you," Taya said after releasing Shawndelle, still holding onto her hand because Shawndelle looked like she was about to pass out. The rest of the congregation was a little bit calmer because Taya had become a regular when she wasn't on the road.

"I'm so sorry. I just can't believe this!" Shawndelle looked up at Taya who was still standing there like it didn't make her uncomfortable at all.

"No worries." Taya bowed her head. "We can get a selfie after service." She squeezed Shawndelle's trembling hand and backed up to the seat beside Chad whose lap was occupied by Patience.

Once things had calmed down and we'd settled into our seats, Daddy came out as ceremoniously as we'd all come to expect, blue robe beaming like a beacon of hope, and the Lord knows that I needed it. Damien hadn't said two words to me beyond hello, and I could feel the tension traveling under the pew like a train on its rails. I avoided looking his way out of fear that those butterflies might start to flutter again. And that'd be highly inappropriate given where we were.

"Good morning, Tabernacle." Daddy's voice sounded as he ascended the set of steps leading up to the pulpit.

"Awwe, we can do much better than that. I said good morning, Tabernacle!" He spoke louder this time and seemingly everyone in the congregation responded, *"Good morning!"* in unison.

"Oh what a blessing it is to be in the house of the Lord." He said, melodically. "Y'all know I'm not gonna keep you long. But I hope you brought a jacket." He panned the crowd, reading glasses hanging from a lanyard around his neck.

"Yeah, I know some of you are looking at me funny. *'Pastor, it's seventy-five degrees outside.'"* He mocked. "But I watched the Weather Channel this morning. Amen?" He panned the crowd again. This time, he widened his eyes.

"And the forecast predicts that by the time we leave this building at five past noon, things ain't gon' be the same outside these doors."

As the congregation absorbed his words, some pulled out their cellphones to validate what he'd just told them. Most of us weren't surprised because, in Texas, we were used to getting all four seasons in a matter of four days. But what I knew to be true aside from my father's observation of the weather forecast, was that it was no coincidence that he brought it up. And it had less to do with his concern for the impending chill catching people off guard and more to do with the word he had prepared for them in relation to the subject at hand.

"Ain't it good to know what's coming, Tabernacle?" He continued, stepping up to the podium and resting his palms on either side of his bible. "Isn't it a blessing to be able to, to, to see what the day's gonna bring before you walk out of your house?" He nodded at all of us.

"But you see, church, we got a problem." He stated with certainty. "Yeah, we got a big problem. Because some of us didn't know about this cold front. Amen?" He nodded his head again and a few sprinkles of Amens came about.

"And it's not because we didn't have access to the information. Amen. It's because we didn't have the time or the desire to look for it." He kept on and you could hear backs straightening and pews creaking as Daddy demanded the congregation's undivided attention.

"If God gave you legs to stand this morning, won't you come and go with me to Matthew twenty-six, verse twenty one?" He requested and a little less than half of the congregation stood to their feet, including Shawndelle, though she didn't have a bible. Luckily, I was standing close enough to share mine.

Daddy read:

"And as they did eat, he said Verily I say unto you, that one of you shall betray me."

He looked out into the congregation before saying, "Jesus knew, Tabernacle. Even while he sat at the table with men that he trusted. Men that he believed to be of good faith. He had a, a, a, a, a forecast." He stuttered. "His Father in Heaven, the weatherman if you will, spoke to him, letting him know that somebody at that table, pulling bread from the same bowl, was gonna cross him. He had a warning. You understand me? But that ain't it. You see, Jesus had some trials coming his way that would've run the average man off. He said in Matthew twenty verse eighteen *'Behold, we go up to Jerusalem: and the Son of man shall be betrayed unto the chief priests and unto the scribes and they shall condemn Him to death. And shall deliver him to the Gentiles to mock, and to scourge, and to crucify him:'*

He stopped reading to look up over the brim of his glasses and ask, "Did y'all get all that?"

One person shouted *"Yes!"* and another *"You better preach!"* both knowing that if Daddy was looking over the brim of his glasses, it was probably about to get serious.

Daddy pulled his glasses completely off and laid them beside his Bible. He didn't need to refer to the *Good Book* for his next words, because they'd be brought to him by way of the Holy Spirit.

"Jesus knew." He said with a certainty that had been handed to him by God. "He was well aware of the forecast before Him. He knew that he would be spat on, called names, nailed to a cross and left to die, because God told him so, Tabernacle. And God is not man that he would lie." Daddy stopped to grab the towel draped over his shoulder and wiped his face.

"But what he also knew," He started with the burning fire of the spirit of the truth lighting his eyes like only the word of God could. "Was the same thing that we all know sitting right here under this roof, safe in his arms, cleansed of all of our sins because they *did* spit in his face and he *was* mocked and scourged and treated like dirt. And as if that wasn't enough for our Lord God to bear, they crucified him and hung him high to end his life forever. Oh, but they didn't believe in a very important part of that forecast, church." Daddy stepped back, throwing that towel back over his shoulder and stepping from behind the podium because he needed space to breathe the word out onto God's people.

My back straightened as his did. My shoulders raised as high as they'd go. I felt a tingle in my throat that was bound to break loose. My Daddy, man of God, father of the truth and nothing but the truth, was about to do what he did best.

"Weatherman said they was gone put Him in a tomb." Daddy started, and the organ player took his cue to play on the rise and fall of Daddy's words. "Said that tomb was gonna be closed and not even the jaws of life would be able to pull it open." He came down one step at a time.

"They thought they had him." He looked up into a crowd of people who were anxiously waiting for him to go where they knew he was going. "One day passed and no sign of Jesus. The tomb was still closed and they were ready to move on. Two days passed and no sign of Jesus. Where is your King they mocked him long. But on that third day!" Daddy shouted and so did everyone else in the church.

I could feel the Holy Spirit walking down the center aisle, laying it's soft but powerful presence over every soul in need.

"My God, on the third day!" Daddy repeated holding a mic to his lips, melodically celebrating the rise of Jesus Christ. "He rose, Tabernacle. Just like he said he would. Just like the forecast predicted, He rose from the dead to secure our faith, and I don't know about you, but I'm so glad he did. I'm so glad he wasn't scared to hang bleed and die for my sins. I'm so glad he didn't act a fool when he knew Judah would betray him. I'm so glad to have a God who saw the storms coming didn't run. I'm so glad to have Him on my side for the rest of my natural life!"

Ushers rushed to the front of the church as a sister on the front pew started to shout and bow her back. From the corner of my eye I could see Damien reacting. And he tried to stay calm, but it was becoming visibly harder.

"God knows what you're going through." Daddy's voice was lighter in keeping with the soft music playing in the background. "He's seen the perils that will come before they even made it to you. Believe me." He panned the congregation, surely connecting with everyone with the sweeping of his eyes.

"And he's here for you." He said, knowing first-hand that the words he was saying were true. "He's here for you and he loves you and he'll see you through. I'm a living witness."

He wiped the sweat beading on his forehead under the bright lights hanging from the ceiling. "Whatever it is that's weighing on your mind. Whatever it is that has you asking why and how long, bring it to God." He stepped beside the altar, having to wait only a moment before five congregants left their seats to join him.

"God has the answer." Daddy continued as more people left their seats en route to the altar. "He is the only one who knows the forecast of your life and he will be right there with you to weather the storm. Bring your burdens to the Lord, my God." He opened his arms, just that quickly finding a third of the congregation at his feet, weeping and pouring out their hearts as the choir softly sang "I Give Myself" away.

I closed my eyes and surrendered to the feeling, feeling Patience's little hand gripping my hand like she always did when she saw me like this. The first time it happened I think it was because it scared her. Witnessing someone surrendering to the Spirit can be a strange thing for a child who can't fully comprehend what it means. But I explained it to her the best way I could. Told her that being filled up with God's presence is similar to being filled up with your favorite meal. It makes you so happy that you might want to cry, and that's okay. It's healthy and helps me to be a better mommy to her and a better person to everyone I meet.

Understanding that discretion was necessary for some in this situation, I tried not to stare when I noticed Shawndelle weeping and leaving the pew out of the corner of my eye. Damien didn't follow her. And that didn't make me feel any kind of way seeing as I didn't really know the dynamic of their relationship. But I couldn't see myself allowing her to go to the altar alone. It didn't seem right considering what she was dealing with. So, led by nothing but the will of God and the goodness that my parents had instilled in me, I caught up to her, gripped her hand in mine and walked her to the altar, heart beating so hard in my chest that it was vibrating down to my fingertips. And so was hers. A pretty face of makeup was almost completely ruined as the tears flowed down her cheeks. I grabbed a handful of tissue off the table at the head of the altar and wiped away her tears, speaking not a single word, allowing the lyrics of the song to speak in our place. I didn't know where this situation was going to lead me or why it had literally been placed at my feet, but if it was in God's will, and it obviously was, I would follow it wherever it took me.

"Are you okay?" Things had gotten so intense that I walked Shawndelle to the powder room after altar call wrapped up.

She wasn't very talkative from what I could see. Or it could've been that she didn't know me.

"No." She shook her head, sniffling and wiping her nose with the Kleenex I'd given her. "I thought I was before I walked in here but apparently, I'm not." She chuckled though it was obvious from the puffiness under her eyes that she was serious.

"It's okay." I took a seat next to her on the fainting sofa, leaning forward and resting my arms on my lap. "Altar call can wring you out sometimes. That's what it's designed for."

"And what comes after that?" She asked as if there were steps to follow. And there were, but I'd never been asked for them in this manner.

"What do you mean?" I sought clarity before I went rambling on and on about how she had to profess her love to God and be baptized and all that.

"I'm gonna die." She plainly stated as if she were telling me about a road trip she was planning to take. "Sooner than I'd like to. And I went to church as a kid a few times, but I don't really have a relationship with God."

Shawndelle's question was clearer with that revelation. And the necessary response was clearer too. "It's never too late to get to know, Him if that's what you're asking." I looked to the side at her, finding her puffy eyes on me and her hands folded together with a soaked Kleenex in between.

"I can't promise you that I'm gonna be here every Sunday." She said. And I appreciated that because honesty was always the best policy. "But I need more of what I got this morning. I need to feel that fullness, so I have something to leave with my son. 'Cause I've never given him anything. Other than life, of course. And if we're being completely honest, I didn't even wanna give him that."

"And why did you?" I asked as if I knew her well enough or had the right to do so. "I mean if you don't mind my asking."

"Because somebody wanted him." She replied, bringing the Kleenex back to her nose. "Somebody loved him enough to beg for his life when I was too selfish to care."

Not many things floored me, especially not at church. But Shawndelle had done so in a matter of ten minutes. There was no need to question who'd petitioned for her son's life because it was evident every time I saw Damien interacting with DJ.

"You're gonna be okay, Shawndelle." I reached over and rested a hand on her knee. "And if you'll accept my help I wanna give it to you. Not just the church stuff but help with your situation as a whole."

She started sniffling again, eyes falling down to the red pumps that matched her black and red knee-length dress.

"Why would you help me? You don't even know me." She looked up into my eyes, a single tear trickling down her cheek.

"I don't have to know you," I replied, fighting back a tear of my own. "I know that God loves you and that's all the reason I need."

I grabbed a bottle of hand sanitizer from the round table on my side of the sofa.

"Here." I opened it and leaned it toward her hand. "I wanna hug you but I'm not tryna get snot on the back of my dress."

She laughed a hearty laugh that she must've really needed. And after watching her smear hand sanitizer on the front and back of her hands, I pulled her into an embrace that ended with the both of us laughing and crying our eyes out.

Eleven

"We need to talk, D."

I'd gone over the conversation in my head at least one hundred times, covering my talking points as well as Shawndelle's because that's the level of pressure I'd put myself under. It'd been almost a week since we visited Angela's church, and I saw a change in Shawndelle that I didn't mention because I didn't wanna make her feel uncomfortable. DJ was still in the dark about why I'd let his mother come back to stay with us after I'd explained to him that she wouldn't be staying with us anymore. He was a good kid, smart as a damned whip. And for some strange reason, I think he sensed that something was different this time.

"Is this about Shawndelle?" He asked, using her government name because to him, my mama was his mama.

"Yeah. Yeah, it is." I sat down on the living room sofa as he stood there in front of me with his hands twisted together.

Shawndelle came in from the guest room where DJ'd helped her put away what small possessions she brought with her for the second time. She eased down onto the sofa beside me, nervous energy rising off a set of shoulders that were already noticeably thinner.

"Why do you look so sad?" DJ asked Shawndelle. And I swear, that put a lump in my throat.

"I'm… *hmm hmm*." She cleared her throat. "I'm not sad, DJ." She reached out and grabbed ahold of his hands, the glossiness in her eyes contradicting her words. "I just get nervous when I have to have big talks. You ever get like that?"

DJ nodded instead of speaking, eyes sliding between mine and his mother's. And as I sat there calculating the weight of the pending conversation, I almost got up and said fuck the whole thing.

But I couldn't.

Because Shawndelle didn't have time for me to be a coward. She could've run off and died without giving her son closure. But she was brave enough to give him what time she had left.

"DJ, what we're about to tell you is… it might be kind of hard to hear." I started the best way I knew how. "And if you wanna cry, that's okay. You know I've always told you that crying is healthy, right?"

"Yes, sir." He nodded his little head, favorite pajama bottoms exposing his ankles, reminding me that it was time to talk him into picking out a new set. "Is somebody gonna die?" He asked as if he was talking about the weather.

"What? Why would you think—"

"He's intuitive." I cut Shawndelle off. "Did you have a dream, D?" I asked because he was always dreaming about things to come and sometimes things that had happened before he was even born. But he rarely saw faces. Just colors or landmarks that connected him to events that he had no business knowing anything about.

"Yes, sir." He nodded.

"Wait, what's going on? Is he psychic or something?" Shawndelle slid forward on the sofa, eyes as big as saucers as they darted between me and DJ.

"Sit down, D." I pulled him to sit between us. "Tell Shawndelle what you saw."

"It was, umm…" He looked up at her nervously before turning his eyes to me. "Remember when Uncle Rudolph died, and he had all those blue flowers everywhere at the funeral?" He spread his arms out as wide as they would go to display the abundance of flowers at my father's best friend's funeral service about two years prior.

"Yeah, I remember." I nodded. Couldn't believe the kid remembered something that happened when he was only three years old.

"I saw that in my dream." He said. "But the flowers were pink. Everything was pink."

"Did you see who was in the coffin, baby?' Shawndelle asked, tears welling in her eyes. This way harder than I'd expected.

DJ shook his head no, and for whatever reason, Shawndelle took a deep breath sending a single tear sliding down her cheek.

"It's ok." DJ turned his body to face hers, using his tiny palm to wipe the tear from her eye. "Paw Paw said good people go to Heaven and Uncle Rudolph was a good person. He always gave me candy and jokes. You wanna hear one?" He asked pulling a smile to Shawndelle's face.

"Yeah." She nodded, cupping her hand over his on her cheek. "I could use a good joke right now, D."

I ruffled my hand through DJ's hair as I stood from the couch, hurrying to the restroom while he started an old joke that Uncle Rudolph must've told me a million times growing up. I could hear Shawndelle laughing from the other end of the hallway while I stood in front of the bathroom mirror thinking about how unfair it was that it took a death sentence for her to see this side of her son. It didn't feel fair, or right, or anywhere close to being beneficial to DJ. But maybe I was just looking at all wrong. Maybe clarity would come before she took her last breath.

Twelve

It was easy to be brave and surrender to God's will until it was actually time to do the surrendering. I'd been setting up appointments for Shawndelle all week, using resources from the centers that collaborated with my nonprofit organization, T.R.U.S.T., for women dealing with postpartum depression and other difficult situations that sometimes came with motherhood. T.R.U.S.T. stood for *time, refuge, understanding, support, and truth,* which were all the things that we offered to anyone seeking our assistance. But as I sat in my car in the parking lot of Damien's condo prepared to walk into this dark situation, I couldn't help questioning whether what I was doing was right, or if it might be easier to pass it off to someone else.

"This is the definition of being a Christian, sis." Jada's voice reminded me that she was on the phone. "We've both seen God line things up for other people. This situation is no different than any other situation he's placed you in."

"But it *is,* Jada." I sighed again. All I'd been doing was sighing the whole ride over and the five minutes I'd been sitting in the car listening to her giving me a pep talk.

"Why, because you like Briscoe?" She mentioned a truth that I was trying my best to shake away. I couldn't ask God to equip me with what it would take to deal with all this with lust lingering in my mind.

"You don't have to answer that." Jada cleared her throat. "Your silence has always been your tell-sign."

"Excuse me?" I pulled the phone from my ear to look at it like it was her.

"Come on, now. Everybody knows it." She chuckled. "You avoid talking about things. Especially when they're true, or difficult, or make you look like a normal human being who fails and falls short of the glory of God."

"That is not true!" I defended. "You make it sound like I'm some goodie-two-shoes."

"If the goodie two shoes fit." Jada chuckled again and she was a second away from me hanging up in her face.

"Listen, all I'm tryna say is you could loosen up a little." She added after making fun of me. "Briscoe seems like a nice guy. And it's obvious that you see that. I mean you wouldn't be going through this for somebody you didn't care about."

"It's not about Damien. It's about Shawndelle and DJ." I turned off the ignition after checking my face in the rearview mirror. "The woman wants to mend the relationship with her little boy and I just wanna help in any way that I can. Everything doesn't have to be about a man, you know."

"I didn't say that it did." She snapped. "But it wouldn't hurt you to include him. He'll be the one picking up the pieces and helping his son to grieve the loss of his mother. I'm sure God would appreciate you being there for that too."

"Jada—"

"I'm not tryna push you up on the brother, Penny. I'm just saying."

"And I appreciate everything that you *just say*," I spoke up. "But I can only focus on one task at a time. Damien's a big boy. He'll be okay."

"And how do you know he's a big boy? You got something you wanna tell me?"

And just like that, her mind had fallen into the gutter, or should I say broom closet. I don't know how we got baptized in the same wading pool and came out so different.

"You know what, bye." I pulled the phone from my ear again.

"Fine. I love you!" She kissed the receiver before I said I love you and kissed it too, ending the call shaking my head and grinning.

It was awkward as hell seeing her under these circumstances. Circumstances that I'd never imagined myself in. Circumstances that I wished weren't real, for my son's sake as well as mine. But there she was, sitting in my living room on the sofa next to my ex, flipping through a bright green planner filled to the brim with appointments that she'd made for a complete stranger without asking for a dime. It felt like I should at least make some sandwiches or put on some music or anything to show how thankful and amazed I was at how generous she was being. Coming from anyone else, I might've questioned motives. But coming from Angela, I knew it was genuine. She could be a little uptight at times but there was nothing fake about her love for God and her obedience to him even after she'd made a mistake.

And speaking of mistakes, it turns out I was one of hers. She hadn't even hinted at us revisiting what we'd done that night and though it weighed on my mind almost as heavily as the situation with Shawndelle, I dare not mention it, sure that she'd see me as an insensitive freak who couldn't put his own desires aside long enough to be there for my son.

I straightened myself and tried to center my thoughts as she left the living room en route to the kitchen where I was standing, pretending to be deeply invested in something on my phone.

"Hey. You okay?" She hadn't asked me that in days. Not since the church visit. And even then, I wasn't sure she wanted to.

"Yeah, I'm good." I lied. I was a fucking mess. And the only thing that would even come close to making me feel better would be a kiss from her lips.

"Wow. That's impressive." She said, leaning against the kitchen counter and looking up into my eyes, a gesture that shocked me.

"What?" I squinted down at her.

"Nothing. It's just, I'd be a mess if I were you." She folded her arms across her chest. "I was so busy making appointments for Shawndelle, I didn't even think to ask if there was anything you needed. So, do you need anything?"

*Hell yeah, I need something. I need for you to stop pretending that just because my terminally ill baby mama came to my house to die, you can't have feelings for me. I want you to stop using God as a wall to place between us when we both know that ain't fair. I want you to raise up on the tips of your toes and kiss my lips so I can have a God damn ray of sunshine amongst all these rainy days. I need **you**, Angela. God, I need you.*

"Nah, I'm good." I breathed out, leaving her standing in the kitchen while I went down the hallway to check on my son. It'd be a blessing if I came out of the other end of this without him seeing the world as a place that is always taking things away and rarely giving us things we can keep. Shit, it'd be a blessing if I could see that for my damn self.

Thirteen

I was gonna go to work that day since work had been the only normal thing in my life for the past two and a half months. Shawndelle had gotten progressively worse and there was an indescribable air of finality hovering over every single inch of my place. DJ'd missed a few days of school, refusing to leave her side, telling her the same Uncle Rudolph jokes over and over again to make her laugh, and in turn, keep her here longer. And I knew this was coming. Understood as an adult that the more time he got to spend with her, the harder it would be to let go. They both discovered how much they had in common during their time together when I was out working and there was no one there but them, Angela and the home health provider. And all of these things were things that I was aware of, like how they both had birthmarks on the back of their right shoulders. Or that they couldn't pronounce shrimp because of the gap between their top front teeth. All of these things were things that I avoided pointing out to my son because I never imagined a day when his mother would be around. Now it'd be all he had left when she was gone, and I couldn't decide if that was a good thing or a bad thing.

"Daddy, come quick!" DJ caught me just as I was about to head out of the door. And as if the high pitch of his voice wasn't enough to tell me exactly what was happening, the look on Angela's face as she stood at the end of the hallway was all the proof I needed.

I placed my briefcase on the dining room table, using all the strength I had to grab my son's hand and allow him to lead me down the hallway. My feet felt like cement and a knot formed in my throat that would break me in half if I swallowed.

I entered the room that Shawndelle and DJ had decorated with all the pictures they'd taken over the past few months and printed out on my office printer. They were both smiling in all of them, even though Shawndelle's body was slowly morphing into something that didn't resemble life at all. The smell of vanilla incense burned like they had been every day since Angela inserted herself into the process of Shawndelle's transition. And though it was a kind gesture that made each morning sweeter for the woman who was lying in my guest bed preparing to take her last breath, I would never be able to smell that scent again without reliving the last days she spent under my roof.

"Briscoe." Shawndelle's voice was barely above a whisper as I stood at the door, paralyzed by the weight of it all, knowing in my mind that for DJ, I had to go through with this because I'd promised him that I would.

I cleared my throat and said, "I'm here." feeling Angela's eyes on me but unable to look at her.

And then Angela squeezed my hand, a silent assurance that she was there for me, void of judgment and fully understanding that I did, in fact, need her.

With the slightest bit of motivation from my son's big eyes, Angela's soft hand, and the literal tiredness rising off of the shell that Shawndelle's body had become, I dragged myself over to her bedside, releasing Angela's hand to hold onto Shawndelle's. She was already cold, breath shallow as her chest barely rose and fell beneath the crisp, white linen sheets that covered her body. Though it was visibly difficult, she brought her eyes up to me, lips parting just enough to say, *'Thank you.'* DJ climbed up in bed beside her when she used what must've been all of her strength to pat the space beside her. And then he lifted her arm and nestled himself under it, resting his head on her chest as she whispered, *'I love you'* slowly and over and over again until she no longer had breath to say anything at all.

Fourteen

The church was about half full of church members who'd gotten to know Shawndelle during the last days of her life. She'd been baptized by my father, refusing his offer to come to Damien's house to do it, insistent on being dipped in the Holy waters of the Tabernacle of Deliverance Baptist Church, no matter how weak she was feeling or how long it took her to walk up to the baptismal pool.

In an act of courage and compassion for his mother, DJ asked if they could be baptized on the same day. Of course, my father obliged, giving them the whole *'Dipping Day'* treatment from the weekend tree wrapping to the personalized stack of pancakes, a treat that Shawndelle was barely able to finish, but tried with a smile on her face.

On this Saturday morning, with the sun shining brightly outside the doors of the church, DJ had mustered that same courage before sending his mother away. He'd told me that she left him a letter and he wanted to read it in front of the church, but he didn't want to tell his father because he was afraid he'd tell him no.

I'd read the letter with him, fighting back tears the whole way through. And the look in DJ's eyes as we sat outside my father's office told me that he could do it because he was the strongest five-year-old I'd ever met.

We walked from the back of the church and up to the podium beside my father, a soft selection playing in the background as people settled into their seats. Damien was front and center, the only semi-family member present besides DJ since Shawndelle had been in the foster system since she was DJ's age, and never settled with a family that wanted to keep her for good.

But we were there. The people who'd taken the time to embrace her and see her through what had to be the hardest time in her life. Damien's face was like stone, only cracking a smile when church members stopped to hug his neck or kiss his cheek after viewing the remains. I found myself staring at him as Chad secured the mic on DJ's collar. I wondered what was going through his mind and how he'd handle things from this day forward.

"Mic check." Chad's voice sounded around the church as he leaned down and spoke into the mic secured on DJ's tiny blazer. He gave a thumbs up and whispered something in DJ's ear that made the handsome little fella smile before descending the steps and leaving him up there with our father.

"Good morning, Tabernacle." Daddy's voice took on a softer tone than usual. "As you all know, we're here to celebrate the life of Sister Shawndelle Parks who gave her life to Christ just a few short weeks ago. Amen?"

We all said *Amen.*

"Amen." Daddy nodded. "Now typically, I'd have a sermon put together to tell y'all about how Sister Shawndelle has gone to be with the Lord and that she's in a better place. But we all know that." He panned his eyes over the congregation. "We've all sat where the bereaved are sitting and one day before it's all over, somebody is gonna be sitting in bereavement of us. Amen?"

We all said *Amen.*

"Well, today, we're gonna do things a little different." He continued, closing the Bible that lay open on top of his podium.

"This morning we have a brave young man who wants to read us a letter that his mother left with him. Is that okay, Tabernacle?" Daddy asked, and my eyes swept straight to Damien as I sat on the first row of the choir stand.

"Go ahead, baby." Sister Bimage spoke up, and scattered words of encouragement came from several pews. But Damien didn't say a word.

"Amen." Daddy nodded, looking down beside him at a miniature version of Damien looking up at him, anxious and seemingly unafraid.

As he unfolded the letter with his tiny hands, I watched his line of sight to see that his eyes were darting between his father on the first pew with his grandparents and great-uncle Charles. Once his immediate family had offered smiles and nods of encouragement, he found Patience who was sitting on the second row with Chad, Jada and my mother who I was finding it easier to look at these days for some reason. Everyone fell silent as the single sheet of notebook paper crinkled in his hands.

Patience yelled, "You can do it, DJ!" Like we were at their school's Field Day, where she'd yelled the same thing every time he participated in an event.

The smile on his face was like a ray of sun shining through the window. And as everyone calmed down from laughing at Patience, DJ mustered the courage to speak.

"Good morning, Tabernacle." He said in a raspy little voice, looking up at my father who was still standing there as a giant, silent support system just in case he needed it.

"Good morning." We all returned the greeting. And my heart was beating so fast for him, you'd swear it was my own child.

"Shawndelle was my mommy but she wasn't always there." He started and I could feel a lump building in my throat. "But that's okay because sometimes people don't know any better and they leave because they get scared."

He swallowed then looked down at his letter.

"She wrote me a letter before she went to Heaven." He continued, and I knew everybody's mind was about to be blown at not only how well this little boy could read, but that he actually comprehended the words because his mother had taken the time to explain what they meant.

He read:

"Dear DJ, if you're reading this letter, it means I'm already in Heaven looking down you. I know that I told you to be brave for your Daddy, but I know that even for a big boy like you, that might get a little hard sometimes. If you're crying right now, it's okay. And if you're not crying, that's okay too. I just want you to know that I love you. And even though I missed out on most of your life, the time I spent with you in our room full of pictures was the best time of my whole life."

He paused for a moment to gather himself, looking out at his father who was still hanging in there while the rest of the congregation was a combined pool of tears.

On a deep breath, he continued:

"There are some people I didn't get to thank enough before I went to sleep, so, I'm asking you to do it for me at the beautiful celebration of life that Miss Angela helped me to plan. First, I want to thank Pastor Fold and everybody at The Tabernacle for coming over and calling to pray with me when I needed it, and more importantly, introducing me to the word of God. I want to thank Angela for sitting beside me every day, brushing my hair, playing music, and listening to my stories even the ones that were not easy to hear. And last, I want to thank your namesake and the best Daddy in the whole world, Briscoe." He took his eyes to his Daddy again before looking back down at the paper.

"He gave me the best gift in the world when he gave me you, and I know he'll continue to take good care of you. Keep on being brave, my handsome little boy. That's me." He pointed to himself. *"I will keep on loving you from way up in the sky. Love, your mommy, Shawndelle."*

You couldn't find a dry eye in the house, except the set belonging to the man who'd fathered the little boy standing on stage. And as we all stood to give DJ a round of applause, I noticed Damien standing up and rushing to the chapel doors, hurrying outside so fast the back of him was a blur.

"Damien!" I knew it was her without turning around. And I knew that if anybody come running it would be Angela because sitting still wasn't exactly her thing.

"Damien, please stop. I'm gonna break my ankles in these heels if I walk any faster." She was closing on me. And the breathlessness in her voice forced me to stop right next to the bench at the head of the parking lot.

"Are you okay?" She asked, blowing out a breath and staring up into my eyes. "I know that had to be hard. I'm sorry I didn't ask you first. But he was so excited, and I didn't wanna—"

"You told him he could do that?" I squinted, lips damn near trembling.

"Not exactly." She sighed. "He sought my advice. The kid's wise beyond his years. You should be proud."

"Yeah, I should be." I shoved my hands in the pockets of my slacks, turning away from her to face the nearly full parking lot. "Woulda been nice to have a warning."

"I know."

"But do you?" I snapped, turning back around to face her. "Do you have any idea how hard this is? How unfair it is that the only solid memories he's gonna have of his mother were on her death bed?"

"Damien, I—"

"You don't know." I cut her off.

Because everybody was seeing the blessing in this and I was still having a hard time. Watching Shawndelle interact with DJ had only put a band-aide on the anger that I knew would come back as soon as she was gone.

"How could you know? You've never gone a day without having everything you need. How could you possibly understand how hard it's gonna be when all of this is over with and I have to go home and watch my son cry himself to sleep every night when he finally realizes that this isn't some play he's participating in? It's real life, Angela. *My* life. And I appreciate all that you've done. But I should've stopped you before it got to this point."

"But you didn't." She stepped in closer, not at all deterred by the bass in my voice or the tension in my stance. "And you couldn't have, even if you tried because it doesn't work like that."

I looked off to the side because when she looked at me, I felt exposed. It's like I was out there naked, and she wouldn't give me my damn clothes. No woman had ever made me feel so bare and so…so fuckin' weak.

"Look at me." Her voice was barely above a whisper, but I heard her loud and clear and still wouldn't look at her. "I need you to look at me, Damien." She tugged at my chin, and with the touch of her hand, that damn lump I'd been avoiding swelled up in my throat.

"I didn't come this far to leave you and DJ. I'm here as long as you need me and even after that. But you gotta tell me that you need me. Or else, how am I gonna know?"

"Typical."

"What?"

"This is typical," I repeated. "I get to break down and worship you while you *'heal me'*, but you get to stay closed up without accepting anything in return."

"This isn't about me." She fumed. The thought of not being needed made this woman upset.

"Yeah, it is. It always is. You're just too self-centered to see it. And I'm over that. Thanks, but I'm over it." I brushed past her in route to the church to gather my son and go home to resume our regularly scheduled program.

"How does wanting to help you make me selfish? I don't understand." She hadn't moved, yelling at me from the other end of the sidewalk.

I slowly turned around, swallowing that lump and willing it to disappear forever, shoved my hands back in my pockets and said, "You wanna be my savior. You wanna be everybody's savior. Because if you're too busy saving us all from our suffering and mistakes, you don't have time to focus on your own shit."

I let my stare linger on her until it made her uncomfortable and she looked away. Her heels came clacking down against the pavement until she was in front of me again, looking back up into my eyes.

"You know what, maybe you're right." She said, lips twitching because it probably physically hurt for her to say that shit. "But that doesn't make me a bad person. That doesn't mean you have to discard me like I'm some piece of trash. I genuinely care about you and your son's well-being and I do not appreciate you twisting my intentions. But if this is how you want it, fine. I'll take my hands off the wheel and you can drive wherever the hell you want."

She put both palms up, backed away and headed off toward the church while I stood there and took a deep breath before heading back in after her.

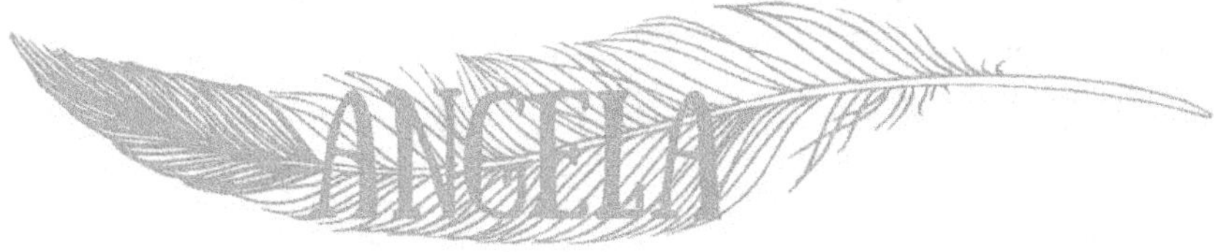

"You *do* have a savior complex. It's not like this is some new discovery."

The nerve of my own sister, sitting at the foot of my bed, passing judgment like I hadn't just treated her to an expensive dinner.

"Why does it have to be a complex because I like helping people? That's the premise of Christianity."

"I agree." She sat up, killing her phone screen after responding to a few comments on her radio show's Instagram page. "But what good is your giving if you're pouring from an empty cup?"

"An empty cup?" I placed my bible on the nightstand, eyes strained and tired from seeking a verse that would help me through this situation.

"Do you have your listening ears on?" She asked, sitting Indian style with her palms pressed on either side of her hips. "'Cause I need you to be open to what I'm about to say and not just listening for an opportunity to speak."

"I do not—"

"But you *do*!" She cut me off. "So, are we listening or waiting?"

"Go."

"That's not an answer."

"I'm listening, Jadalynn. Jesus." I let my head fall against the headboard.

"Good." She bucked her eyes, resting her palms on her knees. "Your heart is big. Everybody knows it and everybody loves you for it. It kind of offsets the fact that you're so uptight."

"I'm sorry, but is this just an opportunity to spew insults or are you going somewhere with this?"

"Both, actually. I mean I love you, sis. But you're wound a little tight."

"Seriously?"

"I said I love you."

"Jada, just get to the point, please. 'Cause I'm itching to punch you in the face right now." She smiled but I was serious.

"Okay." She put her hands up. "What I'm tryna say is that sometimes you get so busy giving that you don't realize you're not receiving. And it sounds selfish, I know. But you gotta let somebody pour into you sometimes."

"I—" I paused because Jada'd made a point and I was legitimately surprised. "Hmm…"

"Is that a good *hmm* or a bad *hmm*? I can never tell."

"It's a good *hmm*," I replied. "Not sure I've ever thought about it like that."

"I'm not sure you've ever thought about it at all." Jada unfolded her legs and slid over to the edge of the bed. "And I hope you will for a little while because it's good for your skin."

"What?" My eyes followed her as she hopped out of my bed and went into my closet.

"Girl, what're you doing!?" I yelled from the bed to the closet, knowing Jada was notorious for stealing my clothes. "There's nothing in my closet that I'm willing to let you seduce Jet with," I yelled again before she emerged from the closet with a familiar golden-yellow dress laid over the front of her.

"Not even this?" She blinked her eyes up from the dress, grinning at me like she knew something she wasn't supposed to know. "Smells like the Sugar Shack. *Strange…*" She dragged, eyes darting between me and the dress that was yanking my mind to the depths of the gutter because all I could remember was how Damien had planted his palms on it, *on me*, before sliding it off of me and…

"Penny?"

"Huh?"

"I've never seen this dress and I've ransacked your closet enough times to have every item memorized. Where'd you wear it?" Jada had let the dress fall over her forearms.

"I don't remember." I slid out of the bed and hurried around to where she was, snatching the dress from her hands.

"I hope Boogie's a better liar than you." She smirked.

"What?" I brushed past her to hang my dress up near similarly colored items because I organized my closet by color in case I woke up blind and still needed to dress my self.

"You're lying. It's written all over your face. And you're a grown woman, so that's pretty damn sad." She stood outside the closet with her arms folded across her chest, waiting for me to come out.

"Did you sleep with Briscoe after the Sugar Shack, Penny? And don't lie to my face because you're terrible at it."

"I…" I paused, so much conflict whirling in my head it was making my temples pulsate.

"Come on. You know how I hate jumping to conclusions."

"First of all, you have a Master's in jumping to conclusions. Second, I don't wanna talk about this. And if you don't mind, I have work in the morning." I stormed out of the closet, then out of the room to go check on Patience before I threw Jada out.

"That's all the answer I need." She was collecting her purse off the kitchen counter when I came out of Patience's room. "And I don't know what you're ashamed of. You needed to be taken care of in a specific kind of way. It makes you human just like the rest of us."

"It makes me sick." I sighed. "I cannot believe I was that weak."

"Penny!?"

"I know." I allowed Jada to pull my hands into hers after dropping her purse on the counter. "I don't even know what came over me. The way he held me when we danced. The way he smelled. The way he looked. It was too much." I dropped her hands and went and flopped down on the sofa.

"Why are you acting like this?" Jada giggled, flopping down on the sofa beside me. "Sis, you deserve to feel all of that."

"But do I? I mean I couldn't even keep a marriage intact. Do I deserve to feel this… this *light* with another man that I didn't even feel with my husband?"

"First of all, yes." Jada craned her neck to look right into my eyes. "And I know we're supposed to guard our temples and all that, but the fact of the matter is that your temple probably hadn't been properly maintained in a very long time."

"Excuse me?"

"You're excused." She smirked. "It doesn't take a dermatologist to notice that glow in your skin after Briscoe popped that coochie. Paul's wack ass could never."

"You know what, it's time for you to go."

"Why? Because I'm telling the truth?" She bucked her eyes, standing from the couch after me.

"No." I stopped to squeeze her hand. "Because your niece's ears never turn off and I don't want her reciting Luke lyrics at Sunday School."

"You're right. My bad." She whispered, looking down the hallway toward Patience's room.

"Anyway, I'm sorry I kept it from you. I just…"

"No worries." She said. "You were just being you. And word of advice—"

"That I didn't ask for."

"That you're getting anyway." She rolled her eyes. "Get you some more of that Briscoe meat. If one dose had you glowing for a whole month, there's no telling what a regular prescription might do."

"Jada, I love you. Now, get your ass out of my house." I picked her purse up off the counter and handed it to her.

"I'm just saying!" She smiled way too big for somebody discussing somebody else's sex life.

"Bye, fool!" I pulled the door open, pressing my hand against the small of her back and gently pushing her out.

"Love you too!" She leaned back and planted a kiss on my cheek before giggling all the way to her car.

Fifteen

"Daddy, are you coming to church with me and Momma? We get graduation gifts today and I want you to see what I get."

A month had passed since the funeral and though Mama and DJ had become regulars at The Tabernacle, I hadn't stepped foot in the church. And it wasn't because I didn't believe in God or anything like that. I just didn't deal with awkward energy well, and if I saw Angela, that's exactly what it would be.

"You can show me your gift when you get home, big head. I got a few things to do around the house." I lied. All I was gonna do was get caught up on Power and eat junk food that I'd have to work off in the gym the next week.

"Okay." DJ wasn't an argumentative kid. And thank God. 'Cause I sure as hell didn't have the energy for it. "Can we go out to eat after church?" He knew he could talk me into just about anything, looking up at me from a set of eyes that were a smaller version of mine.

"Yeah, D." I reached down to straighten his collar, the sound of Mama ringing the doorbell alerting us that it was time for him to

136

go. "Nothing expensive. You've been wearing my pockets out with this fast food all week." I straightened his tie and turned him around to walk toward the door.

"Momma says if you had a woman in here, we wouldn't have to eat out so much." The dude was like a recorder and my mama was always giving him material.

"Your grandma says a lotta things." I shook my head, handing DJ the bible that Pastor Fold had gifted him on the day of his baptism.

"Yep." He nodded, taking the bible from my hands. "She also said that you and Miss Angela would make a cute couple. Whatever that means." He rolled his eyes up to the ceiling, pulling the door open at the sound of Mama's voice fussing about us taking so long.

"Hey, Momma! He's stiffing us again." DJ ratted me out before the door was open good.

"You know you coulda used your key?" I tried changing the subject before it *became* the subject.

"*Or*, you could've opened the door promptly. Preferably wearing a suit." She curled her full lips at the corners. "And good morning, DJ. You look absolutely handsome!" She pinched his cheek and he smiled.

"Thank you, Momma. You look pretty!" The boy knew how to lay it on thick.

"You see that, Damien?" Mama's eyes slid from DJ to me. "Five years old and already knows how to make a woman feel special. I wonder where he got that from?"

"I got it from him, Momma." DJ jumped to my defense. "He took care of Shawndelle when she was sick. If that's not a good man, I don't know what is."

"See." I pulled my son against the side of me and hugged his little shoulders. "What you got to say about that, Ms. Melba?" I hiked a brow.

"He's right." Mama accepted defeat, almost. "But there's another woman, a beautiful god-fearing woman who shall remain nameless, that could use a good man." She winked at me. The woman was relentless. Had been throwing not so subtle hints at me since the day she met Angela.

"She's talking about Miss Angela, Daddy." Even DJ had picked it up. "Can we go now? I don't wanna be late for Children's Church. Patience said we get donuts and chocolate milk today."

"Well, we wouldn't wanna miss that, now would we?" Mama reached out for DJ's hand. "Can't have everybody passing up blessings in this house." She rolled her eyes at me, planting a kiss on my cheek before taking my son off to church.

Daddy'd gone out of town to preach at another church, and service had gone over nearly half an hour due to the notoriously long-winded Deacon Martin taking the opportunity to show off all the sermons he'd been storing away in his fat cheeks. I had watched Jada's entire head open up in yawns at least half a dozen times, and Jet was sitting right beside her knowing exactly why her ass was so tired. And if Chad would've cut his eyes at me one more time while Deacon Martin spoke, I was gonna have to raise a pointer finger and excuse myself from services to step outside and laugh until I cried.

Eventually, the suffering ended, and we were released to go about the rest of our day. I hadn't planned on doing much aside from getting back into my pajamas and falling asleep on the couch while Patience watched the Disney Channel. But just as I backed out of a hug from one of the church members, my eyes swept to the back of the church where my mother stood, holding my baby's hand. And I knew right then and there that sleep and PJs would be the last thing I'd be getting.

Chad, Jada, and Jet made it to her before I did, wrapping their arms around her and the whole nine, making me wish I could disappear. Since Shawndelle's funeral, I'd been telling myself that life was too short, and I needed to at least try to make amends with my mother. But when it came down to it, I honestly didn't know how. So much time had passed and so many feelings had subsided that it almost felt like I'd grown numb to the rift.

"Mommy, can we go to dinner with DJ and his granny?" Patience asked, pulling my eyes away from the wedding ring on my mother's finger that had raised my blood pressure the last time I saw it when picking up Patience, but now didn't anger me so much.

I didn't even realize DJ and Ms. Melba were standing there at the chapel doors until Patience's voice broke me out of my thoughts.

"I… hey, Ms. Melba. How are you?" I asked, putting a hand to my chest, feeling heavy all of a sudden. She and DJ had been in attendance for the past few weeks. I wasn't shocked to see her. I was just in a fog for some reason.

"Hey, honey. Are you okay?" Ms. Melba asked, eyes squinting.

"Ye… yes, ma'am." It felt like there was cotton in my mouth. "I just need to go to the ladies' room. Excuse me." I brushed past all of them without speaking to my mother, hurrying to the restroom to splash some water on my face. I hadn't been around her in so long that her presence must've been affecting me. This had been happening all my life when something was making my spirit uneasy.

"Angela?" A voice that had been the definition of annoyance for the past two and a half years sounded over my shoulder after the bathroom door swung open.

I wanted to shove my head down the drain, and then the rest of my body after that. Anything but being alone in a room with my mother would've made me feel better.

"Baby, are you okay?" She spoke again, leaving me no choice but to straighten my back. I braced my hands on either side of the sink basin, catching her reflection in the wide mirror in front of me, looking like an older version of Jada with hips and lips like mine.

"I'm sorry. I thought you knew I was coming." She said, not moving from where she stood near the door. "I wouldn't't've come if I knew—"

"Stop." I breathed out, blinking my eyes closed. "How else were we ever gonna wind up in the same room?" I opened my eyes and slowly turned around to face her.

"Let's just do it," I said. "Let's just rip the band-aid off right here and right now."

"Penny, you don't have to—"

"Mama, it's been two and a half years." I cut her off. "If it's not gonna happen now, then I don't know when 'cause I've been trying for the last few months to get up the nerve to call you, but I couldn't."

"Okay." She spoke softly, eyes piercing straight through me like only they could, carrying a warmth that I didn't even know that I'd missed because I was too busy denying that it ever existed.

"Do you wanna sit down?" She waved a hand toward the fainting sofa, not taking a step toward it until after I did.

And then she joined me on the silk upholstered furniture that we'd picked out together when Daddy made the mistake of leaving us in charge of giving the church a facelift. My head became flooded with memories of how much fun we had, ripping and running all over Houston collecting pieces that screamed *'Saved and Stylish'* since it was our designated theme. Mama had an eye for colors and patterns that was unmatched by anyone I'd ever met. It was part of the reason I always went with wild color choices myself. It was the thing that made me feel most like her on days when I felt so different.

"I felt that back there." She started where I knew she would. "I've never stopped feeling the shift in your spirit. Not even when you pulled away from me."

God, why'd you have to give me such an intuitive mother? I couldn't even hide from the woman when I was hiding from the woman.

"That's why I rushed down here. Because I knew." She kept on.

"Mama—"

"You don't have to say anything, Penny. The fact that you're even sitting here with me is all I need. Because I love you. And I miss you. And I really want us to fix this."

"Me too," I said, a huge lump forming in my throat, words slipping off my tongue with such ease that I felt stupid for not saying them years ago. "I'm sorry." I looked to the side at my mother, a beautiful woman who had wrapped me up in nothing but love my whole life.

"You don't have to—"

"But I do. So, please let me."

She took a deep breath in then let it out and said, "Ok." Handing me the floor to say all that I'd needed to say.

"When you and Daddy…when you divorced, I felt like the bottom had fallen out of my life." I started. "Like all those pretty words I'd been standing on were lies, therefore making me a lie too. And I resented you for that. I resented you for giving me all of that then taking it away like it never mattered. Like it never meant anything."

Mama didn't speak like most people would when I paused, because she knew me well enough to know that a pause wasn't an opportunity to insert herself. It was my way of gathering my thoughts so that I could present them to her in a way that would be pleasing to God and conducive to our healing.

"I know better than that now." I continued; both of our eyes glossed. "You're human. And I learned that in the hardest way when I had to dissolve my own marriage. Here I was, judging you, and I couldn't even keep my own house in order. That must've been a laughable moment for you."

"No, it wasn't." She squeezed my hand. "And I'm sorry that didn't work out. Actually, I'm not because the two of you weren't even close to being equally yoked. But I digress." She rolled her eyes up to the ceiling before returning them to me.

"Yeah. You might've mentioned that a time or two." I smiled on a deep breath. "Anyway, that doesn't matter. What matters is that I love you and to be honest, I even miss you."

"Miss me? Wow!" She widened those bright expressive eyes that were the first ones I saw every morning before school because Chad and Jada slept until the very last minute, leaving me and Mama to eat together in solitude.

"Yes, I do." I blinked my eyes open to take her in, wondering how in the world I'd done without the energy pouring from her to me for all this time. "And I'm sorry," I said again because I really and truly was. My pain should not have led me to these severely toxic extremes.

"I heard you the first time." She said. "And you don't need to be sorry. You had the right to react however you felt. I'm the one who's sorry."

"For what?"

"For turning you, your sister, and your brother's world upside down. For not using more tact in the situation."

"Mama, you're a lesbian who was married to a minister for thirty-one years. I don't think there was any level of tact that could've made that easy to swallow." I shocked my damn self, saying that out loud. But life had given me so many lessons in such a short amount of time that at this point, there was nothing left to tell but the truth.

"Well, when you put it like that..." Mama shrugged before both of us relaxed against the back of the couch.

"I have been praying for this day longer than I've ever prayed for any day," Mama said, eyes closed as she fell into her thoughts.

"Even my birth?" I rolled my head to the side and watched her eyes pop open.

"Ahh, maybe it's a close second." She smiled, pulling me into a side hug that opened up my heart. Might've even heard Yolanda Adams singing.

We sat like that for at least five minutes, exchanging energy and basking in the spirit of the beginning of healing. It's a shame that it had taken me so long to get to such a seemingly simple resolve. If I had let love lead the way instead of judgment and fear of our family's perfect little image being tarnished, I might've found myself in my mother's arms sooner. Could've saved us both some sleepless nights.

"Aye, y'all good in there?" Chad's voice sounded on the other side of the door just as me and Mama were standing from the sofa.

"Chadwick Fold Jr, how many times have I told you to stop hanging around the ladies' restroom?" Mama fussed as we walked out of the restroom to find Chad leaning against the wall looking nervous as hell.

"Too many." Chad smiled before his face folded in confusion. "In my defense, Jada sent me because she thought there might be a fight to break up."

"Seriously?" I curved my lips to the side.

"What? Y'all been oil and water for a minute." Chad shrugged. "Had to be prepared."

"Well, we're mixing now." Mama gripped my hand as she raised on her tiptoes to kiss Chad on the cheek.

"Good." He nodded, pulling the both of us into a bear hug. "Y'all done stressed me out long enough."

"Boy, shut up and let's go eat." I grinned.

"Yes, let's." Chad nodded. "And speaking of eating, could y'all not sit me next to Ms. Melba? I think she's tryna get at me."

"Boy!" I almost screamed.

"Chad, you need to stop it. That woman's as old as me." Mama fought back a giggle.

"Age ain't nothin' but a number, Mama. She straight up asked if me and Taya were still together. And when I told her we were, she started going on about how she wished she was twenty years younger."

"You are a lie and the truth ain't in you!" My cheeks were sore from laughing so hard.

"Right hand to the Man!" Chad raised a palm. And it took all the strength I had to keep my composure as we rounded the corner approaching Ms. Melba standing at the church entry with Jada, Jet and the kids.

"We'll be sure to sit you on the opposite end of the table," Mama whispered without parting her lips, a trick she had to practice with Jada every time we were around other church folk because Jada's mouth was the least saved part of her body.

"Thank you, Mama." Chad sounded like a little kid. And Ms. Melba was grinning from ear to ear, having no idea how awkward she'd made this brunch gathering by throwing her geriatric box at my little brother.

Lord, help us all.

Mama'd insisted that I meet them for brunch though I'd made it clear that I wasn't in the mood for leaving the house. DJ didn't make it any better, giving me a hard time for missing The Tabernacle's graduate solute. So, I put on some slacks and a dress shirt and took my tired ass down to The Brunch Hut.

The place was packed, as usual. But by the time I arrived, Mama'd shot me a text saying they'd already been seated at the back. I followed the receptionist through a crowd of chattering early-risers, stopping dead in my tracks when I saw what I'd walked into.

"Hey, baby!" Mama was the first to speak. "Come on over here. I saved you a seat." Of course, she had.

Of. Fucking. Course.

"Hey. How y'all doin?" I forced a smile, waving at the table of damn near ten people that I hadn't expected, eyes sliding to Angela who was seated beside my mother with a vacant seat to her left that, apparently, had been saved for me.

"Wassup, Briscoe?" Chad, the closest to the end of the table, stood to shake my hand, as did a man I recognized as Olympic Gold medalist, Andrew "The Jet" Julian.

I didn't have time to be star-struck, too focused on figuring out how to ask my mama why the hell she'd done this without being disrespectful.

Which would be impossible.

Everyone else at the table spoke, including Angela's mother who I was surprised to see based on all that Angela'd told me about their tattered relationship, and her sister, Jada, who was smiling from ear to ear like she knew something about me worth smiling for. DJ and Patience were elbow-deep into some coloring sheets and only looked up from their projects to speak to me for a second apiece as I took my seat at a table full of people who were all a part of a twisted surprise.

"I'm sorry. I thought you knew we were gonna be here."

The waitress had just brought out the last of our plates when Angela decided it was safe to speak under the chatter floating around the table.

"It's all good." I didn't look at her, instead choosing to focus on the grilled chicken breast in front of me.

"But it's not, is it?" She unrolled her cutlery, draping the napkin over her lap. "We're the only two people at this table who don't think we should be talking."

"Talking about what, exactly?" I whispered, still not looking up from my plate. "And how would your mother have a horse in this race? Y'all ain't even on speaking terms."

"We are now." I could see her from the corner of my eye, staring at me as she forked scrambled eggs into her mouth.

"Since when?" I don't even know why I cared. But I did.

"Since this morning. We made amends in the restroom. It was pretty epic. You should've been there."

"Yeah?" I dipped a piece of chicken in my jalapeno grits before forking it into my mouth.

"Yeah." She nodded. "I feel like I'm kind of on a roll, actually." She pulled the napkin from her lap and dapped the corners of her mouth.

"You mind stepping outside with me for a second?" She pushed back from the table and everybody looked toward our end of the table.

"What?" Now, I looked up.

"Come on. It'll only take a minute." She stood from the table and as strange as it felt, sitting there watching her wait for me, it would've felt even stranger not following her lead.

I knew he'd follow me because for as long as I could remember, people found it impossible to tell me no. I didn't take Damien for the type of man to follow orders on a regular basis, by any means. But a lightbulb had gone off in my head after we parted ways and I was gonna continue to lose sleep if I didn't get this off my chest. Dealing with me could be frustrating at times. That, I could admit. Handing over control made me nauseous and opening up made me feel too vulnerable. But being around Damien, watching him soften when necessary despite the obvious comfort he found in being this manly man, I began to reconsider my stance on life in general. Thinking maybe, just maybe, it would be okay to take my hands off the steering wheel.

As we stepped outside of The Brunch Hut, alongside a row of ten-foot hedges away from the listening ears of passersby, I stood directly in front of Damien and looked up into his eyes. He was hesitant to look down at me. So stubborn and hellbent on being right that he couldn't fathom the idea that I'd come out here to tell him he was.

"I know you're hungry. So, I'm gonna keep this brief." I said, nervous as hell about being this direct, potentially handing over even the smallest bit of control to a man I barely knew but couldn't stop thinking about.

"You were right." I started with words that might make him more inclined to listen.

"About what?" He asked. And a sense of relief started to spread from my shoulders down to my knees.

"My *savior complex*." I sighed, feeling the weight of those words as if they were physical beings. "It's the way I'm wired. It's always been my best attribute. And I'll be the first to admit, I don't know how to turn it off."

"It's not your best attribute." Damien shoved his hands in his pockets the way he always did when I'd made him nervous or uncomfortable, which was an extremely huge feat. Because like me, nothing made him nervous.

But I didn't feel like that was the reason for him doing it today. His eyes didn't speak to that truth at all. There was something else controlling those hands.

"I've seen you naked." He bathed me with his eyes, an extremely inappropriate observation that set the back of my neck on fire.

I swallowed. Like a teenaged girl standing in front of her high school crush, I swallowed because I didn't have words.

"What do you want from me, Angela? Why are we standing out here when we both know who you are and that you're not gonna change?"

"Actually, that's exactly why we're standing out here." I dug into the pit of my stomach and found my voice. "I didn't come to this easily because of who I am as a person. But I…"

"You what?"

"I wanna…"

"You wanna what? Is it that hard to say?" He was growing impatient.

"It is, Damien! God, can you respect the fact that I'm trying?"

"No, I can't." He pulled his hands from his pockets and stepped back. "Your efforts are in vain if you don't just do it. Just put all your shit down. Take the fucking cape off and let somebody look out for you."

"I…"

"Just stop talking, man." He took a step forward, planting himself in front of me, body towering over me like a shade tree. "You are many things. Beautiful things. But you know which version of you I like the most? The one that runs through my mind every night before I close my eyes? It's you with your eyes open, staring at me, vulnerable and in need of something that only I can give you. It's you screaming my name like I'm the only man in the fucking world. It's how you feel around me. Against me. On top of me."

He stopped. And I'm sure it was because my mouth was wide open, and my eyes were about to fall out of my damned head.

"I know you probably don't wanna hear that." He sighed. "It's vulgar. Words a man wouldn't dare speak to a woman of God. But it's the truth. The only place I've wanted to be since leaving your body is back *inside* of your body. And I'm sorry if that offends you."

"It doesn't." I responded in a voice that I didn't even recognize. "I mean, it should. 'Cause like you said, it's vulgar. But… God, Damien. What am I supposed to do? Just disregard what I know is right? I can't do that."

"Then don't." His words shocked me, and I thought he was about to walk away. "I'm not asking you to abandon your principles. I'm just asking you to let me have your back."

"Specify." I bit back a smile until I was sure this was something I could submit to without regret.

"You want me to specify having your back? Are you that far removed from using slang, church girl?" He didn't smile but he didn't frown. And for Damien, that was just as good as a smile.

"Trust me to take care of your needs, man." He tilted his head to the side, finding enough patience to break things down for me though I didn't really need it and only asked so that I could see his shoulders tense.

"Which needs?" Now *that*, I did need to know. Because taking care of my body was one thing. A thing that Damien could do without instruction. But there were other parts that needed tending to as well. Parts that had been my responsibility for as long as I could remember.

"All of 'em." He didn't bat an eye, staring at me like he couldn't see any of the bullshit I was carrying around. Or rather he did see it and couldn't wait to take it off my shoulders.

"That's a lot." I hiked a brow, ashamed of how turned on I was on a Sunday afternoon.

"You think I'm not capable?"

"I didn't say that."

"Then let's stop playing games. My track record speaks for itself. I don't play with people and I keep my word. If I say I got you, I got you. Now let's go wrap up this breakfast so I can take care of one of your needs."

"Damien!"

"A blind man can see that your shoulders are tense. And I don't care how much shea butter you work into your skin, ain't shit gon' make you glow like I can."

This negro had abandoned modesty and dived straight into arrogance. And as sad, and filthy, and sinful as it was, I had completely ruined my damned panties.

"What about DJ?" I tried speeding past the shivers in my voice at the thought of him doing me like he'd done me the last time.

"Let me worry about him." He slid a hand under my chin. "I need you just as much as you need me right now." He stared at me for a moment and I couldn't speak through the warmth circling in the pit of my stomach. He stepped in closer to me, roping his arm around my waist, tipping my chin up a little until our lips met in the middle and he swallowed me into a kiss. I forgot that we were outside and in public for the whole world to see. And as I raised up on the tips of my toes to wrap my arms around his thick neck, I didn't even care anymore.

Because he had me.

Literally had me, forming a hedge of protection around my body, and an even bigger one around my soul. I had never felt so understood. So led. So admired in all my days. All I wanted to be was his and all that he wanted was to have me. How could I say no to that? How could I possibly ask for more?

"Wait, what are we doing here?"

Of course, she was surprised when we pulled up to the Sugar Shack. She probably thought we were going back to my place. I could feel the heat swimming from between her legs when I kissed her outside The Brunch Hut and could've easily surrendered to it if

I didn't know better. But Angela didn't need sex and neither did I. It would only be a fog, tricking us into thinking we could actually be together without conflict. I'd tried that with Shawndelle and learned the hard way that it wouldn't work. And I wasn't about to run into that situation again.

"Dancing," I replied, pushing the door open and letting her in first. BB King's voice wrapped around my ears like shelter from the rain. "It's my therapy. Why? Where'd you think we were going?" I looked down at her standing by my side and winked. She rolled her eyes from me to Uncle Charles approaching the counter as I leaned to the side and planted a kiss on her cheek.

"What up, nephew?" Uncle Charles greeted. "And *niece*?" He questioned, pulling a smile to Angela's pretty brown face.

"What up, Unc?" I extended for a dap and hug, stepping aside so that he could embrace Angela.

"How you doin', Uncle Charles?" Angela accepted his embrace like she'd known him her whole life.

"I can't complain." He said as he pulled away. "Y'all pickin' up an order? Tillie got smothered pork chops this evening."

"Nah, Unc. We just came to dance." I said. And I could feel Angela's eyes looking upside my head.

"Ain't nothin' wrong with that." Uncle Charles clapped my shoulder. "Y'all let me know if you need anything. I'll be up here waiting for the crowd to roll in." He nodded then went around the back of the counter to straighten flyers and wipe the phone down.

"Crowd? It's Sunday. Who's coming to the Sugar Shack on a Sunday?" Angela asked as I led her inside the club, locating the table that I'd decided would be ours and pulling out a chair for her to take a seat.

"You'd be surprised." I sat down next to her, quickly approached by a waitress who was dressed more modestly than Sugar Shack waitresses typically dressed.

"Good evening. What can I get y'all?" The young lady asked.

"Two sweet teas, Sarah." I looked up at her name tag since she didn't look familiar. Daddy'd hired some new help for the Sunday crowd.

"With lemon, please," Angela added, squinting at me.

Sarah scribbled down our orders, smiled and walked away, and the look on Angela's face went from confused to more confused.

"What's wrong?" I smiled, barely. I couldn't help it.

"You ordered tea at the Sugar Shack and you're asking *me* what's wrong?" Her brows hiked.

"It's Sunday." I curved my lips. "The Sugar Shack is dry on Sundays."

"So, that's why we're here? To drink sweet tea and dance?"

"Yes."

"But why?"

"Because that's what you need. Did I not just promise to give you what you need two hours ago? And did you not just promise to let me?"

"Yeah. But I thought—"

"You thought I was about to take you back to my spot and bend you over the kitchen sink?" I asked just as the waitress returned with our drinks.

"Thank you." Angela swallowed, feeling seen as hell by the waitress who hadn't heard a word I said under the loud music.

"This is what you *need*, Angie. The kitchen sink is what you *want*." I teased, looking at her over the brim of my glass as I took a sip of tea.

"Whatever." She opened her straw and dropped it in her tea. "You're a tease." She wrapped her lips around the straw and sucked, making my dick jump under my slacks.

"I've been called worse." I grinned relaxing against the back of my seat, legs spread under the table. She couldn't take her eyes off of me and I couldn't take mine off of her. There was a constant pull between us that was stronger than we could resist. But we had to, for the sake of longevity.

"I'm having a hard time sitting way over here without touching you." She said, wearing not an ounce of shame on her face.

And I loved that shit. As tightly wound as Angela was, she was already comfortable expressing her need for me. At least her physical need. But that wasn't gonna be enough. Not for the long haul. Not for the plans I had in mind.

"Come on." I stood from the table then walked around the back of her to pull out her chair.

"What are you doing?"

"You wanna touch me? Come touch me. Horny ass." I reached out for her hand and helped her from the seat, turning around and stepping to the music as Latimore sang *Let's Straighten It Out*.

When we reached the center of the empty floor, I turned back around to find her there following the sway of my steps, smiling so hard I thought her cheeks might burst, showing no resistance as I pulled her in against my chest and rested one hand on the rise of her hip, using the other to drape her arm over my shoulder. We fit like puzzle pieces, and I noticed that the very first time we danced. Instinctively, she followed my lead, because with dancing, if you found the right partner, it just worked that way. I'd been raised up in the Sugar Shack, watching couples dance together for years, seemingly molding into each other, each anticipating the step of the other, knowing without speaking what to do and when to do it. Me and Angela had that. We hadn't even known each other a year, and we had that spark of telepathy on the dance floor that I knew for a fact would never be matched by anyone else. That's why it frustrated me so much that she wasn't the same person off the dance floor *and* outside of the bedroom. That she lost all understanding of being led, and understood, and the all-around freedom of simply being herself not just under my eyes but under the eyes of the world. I needed her to see that perfection was a myth and the only thing that either of us could be sure of was that we had chemistry and no matter how great or small our flaws were, that wasn't something that could be manipulated. It was there for a reason and we had to figure out the in-between. Two strong personalities had to find compromise for the sake of what could turn into love.

"Damien?" Her words bathed my neck.

"Wassup?" I looked down into her eyes, trying not to shiver because I'm a grown-ass man.

"This feels good."

"I know."

"But how? How do you know?" She asked, full lips begging me to kiss them.

"Because it's supposed to," I replied, tightening my hold around her waist. "It's all right here." I applied pressure to the small of her back. "I can feel you. Lead you anywhere from right here. And do you know why?"

"Please, tell me." Her lashes fluttered as she waited for my reply.

I pulled her so snug against the front of me that I could feel her nipples pebbling beneath the silk fabric of her blouse, and her eyes told me that she could feel me hardening against her belly. "Because you want me to." I declared what she already knew to be true. Angela desired being submissive. She'd just never met a man worth submitting to.

Neither of us said another word as the next song came on, choosing instead to let the lyrics and the instruments speak in our place as we blazed a trail on the dance floor that no one else could stand in. With her body nestled comfortably against mine, the energy of restraint slowly melted away. I looked down to find that her eyes were closed which meant that she was feeling without the need to see and didn't care who was watching.

And that was a good thing.

Because had she seen our people walking into the club still wearing their Sunday best, she might've fainted the same way I did when I walked into The Brunch Hut and saw the same thing. I figured one surprise deserved another. And every Sunday was Family Day at the Sugar Shack. It's like God had laid the whole thing out. It couldn't have been more perfect if I'd planned it a month in advance.

"That church coochie must've been the best he ever had." Jada's foul mouth never took a day off. And instead of focusing on the fact that both of our parents were on the dance floor with two people that were not our parents, she chose to corner me while I called myself ducking off to take it all in.

"I'm not entertaining you right now, Jadalynn." I rolled my eyes from her back to the dance floor where Chad, the only one without an adult dance partner, was holding Patience and DJ by the hands, spinning them around in circles.

"You don't have to." She smirked. "This is entertaining enough. You gotta be sittin' on some millionaire dollar vagina to get a man to pull off something like this. He got the pastor *and* his ex-wife in the Sugar Shack on a Sunday, dancing to Johnny Taylor like the Lord ain't lookin'. That's some good shit, sis."

"You know, every night I pray that you don't go to hell." I shook my head at my sister who was laughing in my face. "I might make some prayer adjustments tonight, cause you are really getting on my nerves."

"I love you too!" She leaned in and kissed my cheek, roping her arm around the back of me.

"Whatever. Where's Jet? I need to be saved from you right now." I folded my arms across my chest just in time to have my mind blown when Mama and Daddy switched partners, leaving them dancing with each other while Sister Bimage and Mama's Manny Fresh looking wife danced together.

"In the restroom," Jada replied. "And let me go find him before our parents invite him into this swingers club."

"Jada!"

"Girl, I'm playin'." She elbowed me before heading off toward the restroom. "Loosen up. The Fold is expanding, sis!" She yelled over the music, winking at me and disappearing down the hallway, swaying her hips to the music.

"You alright over here?" A deep voice sounded over my shoulder, sending chills down my spine that I couldn't help reacting to.

"Yeah," I answered with warmth crowded my senses as he pressed against the back of me and wrapped his arms around my waist. "Just waiting for the shock to wear off. I can't believe you did this."

"You mad?" His voice vibrated against my neck, smooth lips kissing my sensitive skin.

"As much as I wanna be, I'm not."

"And why would you wanna be?" I could feel him smiling with his chin resting in the groove between my neck and shoulder.

"'Cause I didn't put this together and I'm used to being the one who puts everything together." I pouted like a big baby.

"I'm sorry." He kissed my cheek. "But if it's any consolation, it was way harder than it looks. All the people on that dance floor, including the smallest ones, are difficult as hell."

"No way!"

"Yes, way!" He mocked. "And to make things worse, I think my mama got a thing for your brother."

"Damien, if you don't stop playing with me." Now I had to turn around and look him in the face.

"Right hand to the man." He pulled an arm from around my waist to raise his hand.

"We gotta do everything in our power to make that stop because it is gross."

"Who you tellin'?" Damien squinted. "I'm all for Stella getting' her groove back. But Melba needs to leave her groove the hell alone."

"Amen?"

"Amen!" We both laughed until one of the little people wandered off the dance floor and found their way over to us.

"Why are y'all dancing in the corner?" Patience looked up at us and asked, yellow ruffles catching flickers from the strobe light. "Come dance with everybody else. Uncie Chad said he's gonna teach us how to do the Cupid Shuffle!"

"Alright, baby. Lead the way." I took Patience's hand. "Damien, you comin?" I looked back at the handsome mound of chocolate that had come in to rearrange my life.

"I'on't know. Y'all got enough room?" His eyes slid from me to Patience. And something about the way he asked that question made me think that he was asking for way more than space on a dance floor.

"Yes!" Patience replied without hesitation, a smile spreading across her face that made her little eyes squint. "Just follow me. I'll show you where to go." She reached for Damien's hand and he gladly took hers, following her onto the dance floor where our family circus was waiting.

Epilogue

One year later...

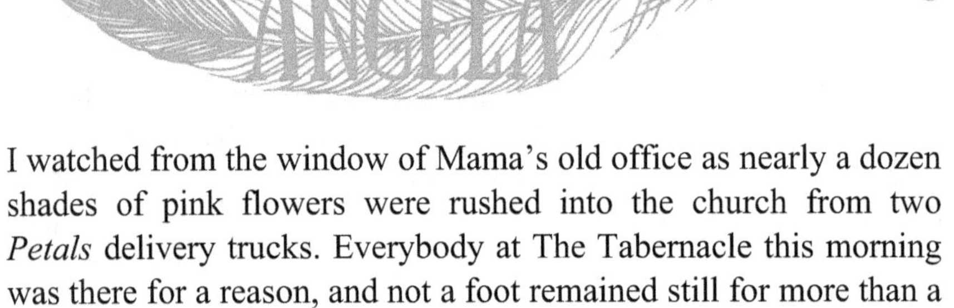

I watched from the window of Mama's old office as nearly a dozen shades of pink flowers were rushed into the church from two *Petals* delivery trucks. Everybody at The Tabernacle this morning was there for a reason, and not a foot remained still for more than a minute at a time. Orders were being yelled from one hallway to the next. And even the kitchen staff, who usually ran their own show, had to share their space with the hired caterer. A three-foot-tall cake anchored the space with folks carefully maneuvering around it, bearing in mind how many man-hours the *Brothers Three Bakery* had put into bringing the creation together. It was the busiest I'd ever seen the place. You could feel the excitement vibrating against the walls. It was a very special day for the Fold family. And everybody who was anybody would be there to watch.

"You okay over there?" Jada came in from out of the powder room after getting her make-up done. I turned from the window to face her and had my breath taken away.

"Am *I* okay?" I pressed a hand to my bare chest, pointer finger landing on the diamond neckless that she'd gifted me and Taya, her only bridesmaids. "Jada, you look beautiful!" A chill ran down my spine at the sight of my little sister in her wedding dress. I had never seen her look more gorgeous. I had never felt more emotional.

"Stop it! You're gonna make me ruin my makeup." She footed over to me, the four-foot train of her cream-colored, strapless gown trailing behind her.

"I'm sorry. I just…I've never seen you look this angelic. Like *ever*!" I widened my eyes and we both laughed.

"Forget you!" She trailed from her giggles, looking down at the gown that me, her, and our mother had fallen in love with after visiting three different bridal shops and trying on fifteen gowns.

Taya's mother, Tashena, referred us to a flourishing boutique called *Spectrums* that catered to women of color. From the handmade head-dress down to the custom four-inch pumps that were draped in the exact same silk that Jada's dress was made from, not a detail was left unnoticed. Every time I looked at the dress, I saw something beautiful and new.

"What do you think Andrew's doing right now?" Jada asked, stepping up beside me and looking out the window. And before I could say anything, someone knocked at the door.

"I bet the answer's in here." Taya pulled the door opened and accepted a pink box from one of Jet's groomsmen with a small envelope on top. "It's for the bride." She smiled, walking over to me and Jada wearing a pale pink dress similar to mine, with off the shoulder sleeves where mine was sleeveless.

"Thank you, Taya." Jada accepted the box with a smile. "I'm scared to open it. He's been pranking me all week."

"Pranking you how?" Taya took a seat on the sofa by the window.

"Yeah. I kinda wanna hear this." I smiled at Jada.

"Monday morning, this fool sent me a text asking if it would be okay if Miss Opal moved in with us," Jada said, still holding the box like it had a bomb in it.

"Are you serious?" Taya chuckled.

"Dead ass," Jada replied.

"And what'd you say?" I was almost one hundred percent sure it was something smart because that's just how Jada operated.

"I said hell no. Duh!"

"Jada!" I covered my mouth, though I wasn't at all surprised.

"What? Miss Opal makes sandwiches all damn day. Just spreading Miracle Whip and waiting for somebody to show up. I don't need her roaming around the house in that cowboy hat, fattening me up like those horses in her stable."

"Lucy Pearl and Larry are thick as hell." Taya laughed.

"Jada, that was mean. What if he was serious?" I stepped up behind her to straighten the train flowing from her headdress.

"Then we may not be standing here right now." She said without flinching. "Open this for me." She looked over her shoulder at me.

"Are you really that scared to open a box?" I asked.

"Yeah. What if it's a flower that squirts water or something? You saw how long I was in there getting this face beat. I literally don't have time for Drew's shit right now."

"And I do?" I hiked my brows.

"Oh, give it here. I'll open it." Taya hopped up and snatched the box and envelope from Jada's hand, opening the envelope and immediately clutching her chest.

"What's it say?" Jada's voice hiked, eyes wide open with curiosity that she wasn't brave enough to satisfy for herself.

"Nothing," Taya said. "Just that *he's glad he was finally able to run you down. And it was worth every single sprint.*"

"Oh my God! Is that really what it says?" Jada sniffled, taking the card and the box from Taya's hand.

She opened the box and her face instantly folded, a single tear trickled down her cheek and I was right there with a Kleenex.

"What is it, Jada?" I dabbed her cheek before her blush was ruined.

"This." Her voice cracked, lips trembling as she showed me a blinged-out asthma pump with a note attached that read:

"Meet me at the altar. And please bring this for when you take my breath away."

It was an inside joke that only the two of them could appreciate and that was the definition of love. Getting each other in the simplest of ways.

I could feel my heart beating through my clothes and the inside of my mouth was as dry as the Sahara. Nobody but the bride and groom knew what had me standing on the side of the dance floor with sweaty palms since I'd told them out of respect, not wanting to take the spotlight off their special day. Pastor Fold had given me his blessing, of course. But he didn't know the details on when I'd be popping the question. Things had moved so fast, from the vows at The Tabernacle to the reception that had stopped traffic with all the guests traveling from the church to Jet's grandmother's ranch with police escorts at the front and back end. It seemed like somebody somewhere was messing with the clocks. It could've been the excitement of it all, seeing so much love in one space. Or it could've been that in a few short minutes, the spotlight would be on me.

Everyone who was anyone was in attendance at Jet and Jada's wedding. From radio personalities that I didn't recognize until they spoke, to H-Town's Favorite Nephew, Kenny "Plus" Washington. I'd never been in this situation or anything similar to it. But it helped that although these folks were well-known individuals, they were as laid back as they come blending into the scene like nobody in the world knew their names.

"You okay? Lookin' a little pale over here." Angela came back from making sure Patience and DJ hadn't talked Chad into giving them a third slice of wedding cake.

"I'm good." I looked down into a set of brown eyes that made me feel more seen than she could possibly know. "Just waiting for my chance to get you on that dance floor," I added flirtatiously, watching her body react with a slight shiver that I'd come to expect.

"Just say the word, Mr. Briscoe." She hiked a brow.

And I seamlessly tipped my chin at Jada who was sitting at the center of the head table, waiting for my signal. She nudged Jet who was sitting right beside her, and he left the table to hurry over to the DJ booth. It was like a chain reaction and I couldn't believe it was happening, although I'd gone over it in my head at least one hundred times.

"Party people, can I have your attention?" The DJ, Jada's radio co-host Squeeze, came over the speakers.

"We got a special request coming from the head table. Can I please get Briscoe and Angela to the dance floor? Briscoe and Angela, you have been summoned to the dance floor!"

Angela's eyes flew straight up to mine. I shrugged my shoulders and pretended not to know what was going on.

"If you got warrants, I'd strongly advise you to take the rear exit as fast as you can. Security is looking directly at you, bruh." Squeeze joked and everybody started laughing.

"Are we runnin' or what?" I looked down to the side at Angela who was still looking confused. And rightfully so.

"Damien, what is going on?" She whispered through tight lips with every eye in the reception hall on us.

"How about we go to the floor and find out?" I laid my hand out, and she hesitantly laid her hand in it, following me to the center of the circular dance floor as the lights dimmed around the room, leaving a single spotlight over the two of us.

I swallowed.

The lump in my throat was so fat that it almost hurt but I swallowed because it was in the way of my words. Before I could speak, I scanned the room to find our children. I needed to see their little faces to remind me of the enormity of the commitment I was about to make. And when I found them to my right, each holding tight to Chad's hand, I was centered. Still nervous as hell but centered in my own thoughts. I had never felt a greater love in my entire life.

After watching the day fly by at lightning speed, suddenly everything seemed to be moving in slow motion. I swept my eyes from the kids back to Angela, and my heart skipped a beat. She was glowing it seemed. Kinky crown rounding her pretty brown face. Bare shoulders glowing beneath the cream-colored light. She was perfect in a way that she would never understand. Not only to my eyes but more so to my soul.

"Damien?" She whispered again, eyes seeing right through to the heart of me as she realized what was taking place.

"Angela, I love you." I started, hoping my voice wasn't shaky because I really couldn't tell. "I'd say I knew that the first time I saw you. But your sister was there, and she knows that's a lie."

Jada laughed out loud as did everybody else.

"Some things you have to grow into." We both smiled at each other. And I swear I felt myself falling into the floor when her cheeks pushed her eyes into a squint.

"I've been going over what I was gonna say tonight for longer than I care to admit." I continued. "But now, I can't remember any of the words on the paper in my pocket because looking at you... Baby, looking at you always scrambles my thoughts."

I felt the shiver in my voice that time. And what I felt next was a tear sliding down my cheek before Angela ran her thumb across it.

"Sorry, y'all. I just... I love this woman." I wiped the other eye, then grabbed her hand and kissed it.

"That's alright, brother!" Pastor Fold shouted.

"Ain't nothin' wrong with it, nephew!" Uncle Charles joined in from behind the bar that Jada and Jet had hired him to tend because they'd grown fond of his antics during our nights out at the Sugar Shack.

"Now that the elders have voiced their approval," I smiled at Pastor Fold and Uncle Charles, sending a ripple of laughter throughout the crowd.

"Angela Gisselle Fold," I held onto her hand and went down on one knee, thankful as hell that I wasn't mic'd up or everybody would've heard my knee crack. "Will you please dance with me for the rest of my life as my wife?"

The tear falling down her cheeks was all the answer that I needed. But it didn't hurt to hear her say "Yes!" at the top of her lungs.

So caught up in the moment, I'd forgotten the ring in my back pocket until DJ shouted, "Daddy, you can't propose without a ring!"

He'd played me big time and had everybody laughing as I pulled the ring out and watched Angela's eyes light up as I slid it onto her finger, nerves calmed by the warmth of her skin.

"Get up here!" She stared down at me and tugged my hand until I stood, void of words to express how she was feeling. But it was written all over her face and sweet on the brim of her lips as I took her into my mouth and kissed her like no one was watching though everybody was.

"You're gonna go blind if you keep staring at that thing."

Damien was probably right. I'd been sitting on the sofa with my feet propped on a pillow, wearing nothing but one of his T-shirts and a brand-new engagement ring since the kids were with Chad and there was really no need for clothing.

"I can't help it." I glanced over the back of the couch at him in the kitchen putting away the last of the plastic bowls and cups that DJ and Patience had put in the dishwasher that morning before the wedding.

"I literally would've walked into the jewelry store and picked this exact ring. It's like you're psychic." I brought my eyes back to the three-carat solitaire that couldn't have been more perfect if I chose it for myself.

"Actually, Chad's the psychic." Damien turned off the kitchen light and joined me in the living room after lighting a *'Briscoe'* candle from the new line of scented products that I'd added to my line and named it after him because the scent was masculine and intoxicating.

"Yeah. But you were smart enough to ask him." I smiled up at the handsome object of my affection. "As long as the words inside the band were yours, we're good."

"What? *'Love is patient and we are proof'*? Who else would know that but me?" He grinned. He'd been doing that more often these days.

"I still owe you a smack upside the head for that one." I rolled my eyes back down to the ring, moving my legs from the pillow when I thought he was about to take a seat. But instead, he ordered Alexa to play "Steady Love" by India Arie.

Our song.

"Damien, what are you doing? Haven't we danced enough tonight?" I folded my arms across my chest, body conflicted between going to sleep or doing whatever Damien had in mind.

"No." He extended a hand to me, waving his hips from side to side, knowing how easily that enticed me. "I'm tryna get forgiven. Come on." He flipped his long fingers, giving me no choice but to get my whipped ass up off the sofa.

"We got this whole place to ourselves. How often does that happen?" He asked. We'd been splitting residences for the past couple of months, spending a few nights at his place and a few nights at mine to get the kids acclimated to this new family dynamic.

"Never." I sighed, accepting his hand as he pulled me up off the sofa with little to no effort. "And I'm still a little salty about the kids spending the night at Plus's house. I actually know the words to his songs. It kinda doesn't seem fair when you think about it."

"I don't know what surprises me more. The fact that you know Plus's songs or the fact that you're jealous of a six-year-old girl and a seven-year-old boy." Damien pulled my arms up around his neck and roped his arms around my waist.

"Judge me all you want," I smirked, lips so close to his that I could kiss him. "But if those brats come back home bragging, I'm confiscating their tablets."

"Now that's just mean." Damien's broad shoulders slumped as he guided our steps from side to side.

"All is fair in love and war," I added, cheeks warming, heart fluttering as he leaned in and kissed my lips.

"That's what they say." He smiled without parting from my lips, squeezing me so tight I could feel his heartbeat and his flesh hardening against my belly.

"Feels like somebody's ready for war right now." I loosened my arms around his neck to lean back and slant my eyes down at his crotch. "You want war with me, Mr. Briscoe?" I dragged my eyes back up to his and found them there looking hungry as hell.

"You see the weapon." He glanced down at his dick then back into my eyes, knowing full well that dancing always led to this if the kids were asleep. And would be even more eventful with them gone for the night.

"I got one too." I grabbed ahold of his wrist and guided his hand down between my legs.

I rolled up the hem of the T-shirt I was wearing, barely leaving a shadow over my pantie-less prize. Biting down on my bottom lip,

I kept my eyes fixed on Damien's because he loved the way I looked at him before and during sex. He didn't hesitate to sink a digit inside me, pulling a moan from my mouth when he broke the barrier of my slick folds. My belly filled with heat and a heaviness settled in my chest that made it hard for me to breathe, and even harder to remain standing. He shoved his fingers inside me, and I instinctively parted my thighs, roping my arms back around his neck to stop myself from falling.

"Aah aah!" I moaned, rocking my hips against his palm, lips falling open and staying that way as he took my breath away.

Damien didn't make a sound. Just stared at me, watching me fall to pieces just that quickly from the power of his touch.

"Alexa, play it again." He said, still fingering my pussy, still staring at me possessively. As if we didn't have enough of a connection to this song after dancing to it at least once a week, he was gonna make me cum while standing in my living room with the damn song playing in the background?

On the tips of my toes, I nearly begged for mercy. I couldn't handle being this close to climax with my toes digging into the carpet. He pulled up, anchoring his fingers so deep inside me, thumb circling my clit, applying way too much pressure. There were words in my head that wouldn't come out of my mouth because I was in an intense battle between speaking and breathing. And he was just staring at me. Beautiful brown face still and present as if what he was doing to me wasn't a chore but a duty that he took so seriously that he didn't even care to take care of himself until I'd gotten what I needed.

And I did.

Shivering like an idiot when he found my spot and tapped against it over and over and over again, holding me in place against his bare chest when my legs turned into useless instruments that were no longer able to hold me upright.

I'd found more explanations in Angela's eyes than I could ever ask for from her lips. And she would try to close them when I was deep, deep inside her, but I wouldn't let her because they were saying shit then too. Like how she hated being seen as vulnerable or in need of anything when it was obvious from the moans from her lips to my ears that she needed the shit out of me. And I needed her too, inside and outside of our bed. She challenged me in a way that I didn't know was necessary for a man who was always in control of everything.

"Baby." She sat up on top of me, squeezing tight around my dick, having no idea the lengths I'd go to keep that smile on her pretty face.

"Yeah?" I pushed my hips up from the bed, drilling into her deeper, watching her breasts bouncing under the glow of the candle flickering on the nightstand.

"I love you." She purred, head falling back, eyes up to the ceiling as she ran her fingers through her hair to ground herself because she'd told me before that having me inside her made her feel like her soul might detach and float away.

But it wouldn't.

Not while I was beneath her, or on top of her, or inside of her, or anywhere near her. Because I loved her too much to let parts go missing. Especially my favorite part: her spirit.

"I love you too, baby." I groaned, completely abandoning the part of me that was masculine and dominant, taken over by the strength and beauty that was riding my dick.

"Fuck me." She begged, eyes returning to the penetrative stare that only she could give. "Please, baby. Make me cum!" She pulled her bottom lip between her teeth, leaning forward and planting her palms on my chest, sliding up and down my length until I damn near screamed.

I planted my hands on the rise of her hips, controlling the rise and the fall and the rhythm of the stroke. Breathlessly she pled for me to go harder. And without hesitation, satisfying needs of my own, I slammed into her hard enough to push her eyes wide open and a panting scream from her lips as she slid her hips back and forth.

"Fuck, Angie!" My knees fell to the side. I released her hips to grab her titties and pull them against my lips.

Her ass slapped against my thighs as she rode me faster and harder, sending my fucking head spinning and my dick jumping inside her, painfully swollen with the need to release.

I fell back against the pillow and pushed my hands behind my head because I couldn't take this shit. It was damn near too much. The way she threw the pussy forward then slid it back. The way her face contorted like she was ready to cry. The way her belly caved and expanded when I was deep inside it, and she leaned back to plant her hands on my thighs. I was coming undone from the inside out. I needed to release so fucking bad I was losing my damned mind.

"Damien!" She cried, ass slapping against my thighs. "Baby, I'm gonna. FUCK!" She screamed loud enough for the neighbors to hear from five damn blocks away.

I pushed and pumped and stroked that pussy as hard as I could until the walls started crashing around us and I overflowed between her legs.

"God." She blew out a breath, still on top of me, soaking wet around me, pushing her hair out of her face as she sat up straight with an exhausted smile on her face.

"I can't believe we get to do this shit for the rest of our lives." Her brows hiked as she panted, remnants of climax sending a shiver through her body that caused her titties to jiggle and my dick to jump inside her.

"Already?" She bit down on the corner of her lip.

"For life is a long time. If you tired already—"

"Don't play with me." She halted my words with a finger to my lips, followed by her easing up off my dick, before sliding right back down again.

The end...

More stories by Sabrina
Lena
Yours Truly… Or Something Like That (Book One)
Bodies: Secrets, Flesh, & Blood (Book One)
Bodies: Black & Blue (Book Two)
Bodies: Carried Away (Book Three)
Stone Bodies Productions: The Grind (Book One)
Stone Bodies Productions: The Fall (Book Two)
No Love (A Story Of Love Avoided)
The Lake (A Novelette)
Butterflies In A Mason Jar
So This Is Christmas? (A Novel)
Shaw Siblings After-Words: Keys And Choruses-Jordyn
& Russell (Book One)
Shaw Siblings After-Words: Addicted-Jessie & Chloe
(Book Two)
Shaw Siblings After-Words: Separated-Josh & Simone
(Book Three)
A Scattered Life Series: Six Marble Headstones (Book
One)
The Bricks: Apt. B17 Camille (Book One)
The Bricks: Apt. F53 Tasia (Book Two)
The Bricks: Apt. F58 Keshia (Book Three)
The Bricks: Apt. A1 Freddie (Book Four)
A Collection Of Christmas Stories From The Bricks
Petals
The Color Spectrum Duet: Ivory (Book One)
The Color Spectrum: Ebony (Book Two) By Chencia C.
Higgins
How To Love
Who To Love
Naughty: An Erotic Christmas Novella
Nasty (An Erotic Spin-Off)

Plus
The Fold Thou Shall Not Run (Book One)
The Fold: Thou Shall Not Hide (Book Two)
Freaky Tales
Desdemona's Closet: A Christmas Tale

To the readers…
Thank you so much for taking the time to read this story.
I hope you enjoyed reading it as much as i enjoyed
writing it!

For more of my stories, please visit my author page
On Amazon Sabrina B. Scales

Please, rate and review.
It's the best gift any reader can leave for an author,
Worth more than its weight in gold!

For Inquiries, Please Contact Me At:
Sabrinabscales@Gmail.Com
Or
Like us on Facebook Author Sabrina B. Scales
Or
Join us in The Bricks Reading Group
Or
Follow us on Instagram @Auhtorsabrinabscales
Thanks a bunch. Keep reading!